People

William Halliday

MAPLE
PUBLISHERS

People Power

Author: William Halliday

Copyright © William Halliday (2022)

The right of William Halliday to be identified as author of this work has been asserted by the author in accordance with section 77 and 78 of the Copyright, Designs and Patents Act 1988.

First Published in 2022

ISBN 978-1-915164-54-4 (Paperback)
        978-1-915164-55-1 (Ebook)

Book cover design and Book layout by:

    White Magic Studios
    www.whitemagicstudios.co.uk

Published by:

    Maple Publishers
    1 Brunel Way,
    Slough,
    SL1 1FQ, UK
    www.maplepublishers.com

CONTENTS

Chapter 1 4

Chapter 2 14

Chapter 3 26

Chapter 4 42

Chapter 5 55

Chapter 6 64

Chapter 7 80

Chapter 8 92

Chapter 9 102

Chapter 10 115

Chapter 11 128

Chapter 12 138

Chapter 13 153

Chapter 14 164

Chapter 15 173

Chapter 16 189

Chapter 17 197

Chapter 18 207

Chapter 19 216

Chapter 20 227

Chapter 21 237

Chapter 22 246

Chapter 23 249

Chapter 24 256

Chapter 1

He was stronger than he ever imagined. He told himself that you don't know how strong you are until strength is all you have left. Since he had witnessed his younger brother almost destroy his own life, he had coped well. Steven often asked himself if he could have done more to help Ryan in his time of need.

Steven Walker had been a laid-back character, the type who took everything in his stride. Nothing got him down. He had maintained a positive attitude in life and knew that, when feeling down, it was only a matter of time before the positives returned. Because he had watched Ryan suffer from severe drug abuse and mental illness, his outlook on life had changed. Now he had a *live for the day* attitude.

At thirty, Ryan struggled with addiction. This was hard for Steven to deal with despite them having had a close relationship back when there was nothing to worry about; they had been kids just being kids. They had created fantastic memories during their exceptional childhood, but the brother he knew then was long gone. A few years ago, he would have sold Steven's dog for ten pounds to buy more drugs if given the opportunity.

As he sat on a broken bench in an abandoned kids' playground, Steven gazed across the open fields. Trees surrounded the vast circular boundary. A playground, which hadn't seen a child in years, had become a no-go zone for the youngsters because of intelligent parenting. He thought about the occasion he found Ryan there, in a state of overdose.

'What if I hadn't been around that night?' he said out loud to himself.

There were so many what-ifs and buts.

Castle Drum Park was the chosen location for drug dealers to hang around. It was ideal for them because of the wide-open space, making it difficult for any surprise police busts. The officers had eventually given up trying to control the situation and left them to their own devices, even if it meant breaking the law.

Ryan Walker had made good progress the last time he met his Steven at the park. That had been the area responsible for the downward spiral for him and many others from the area. Some lads never even made it into their twenties. Steven was good friends with the same crowd as Ryan, but he was aware of the consequences of getting involved in heroin. He had started and finished with weed, and that was enough for him; a smoke of the green. It opened his mind and accessed his higher-level thought process more than usual. The silly things he had done when stoned, like putting his phone in the fridge instead of returning the milk, were insignificant. Some people called weed a gateway drug that would eventually lead to other things, but it was no such drug for Steven. He had the strength to say no and felt guilty that he hadn't talked sense into Ryan. At the last visit, his brother was suffering from depression and mental illness.

'It's not my fault,' Steven had reassured himself.

Stretched out along the damaged park bench, he took up its entire length. At six foot two, he had to bend his right leg to get comfortable. Medium build, with longer than average dark hair, some people had commented he was the double of Richard Ashcroft from The Verve. Steven had liked that because Ashcroft was hip and trendy. He shrugged it off with a slightly shy smile.

Overthinking brought his mood down, and he was aware of it. So, it was time he moved on from the shithole of a park and created some more positive thinking. He had made something of his life, not much, but better than most of the crowd he used to socialise with. He had a habit of using his fingers to count how many people had survived the housing estate. Many were dead, in prison, had illnesses, and only a few had jobs. It was not the best of places, but it was his place and a place where many decent people grew up. He wouldn't change it for the world.

He was one of those decent people, and he owed this to his father, who had been the proprietor of a reasonably sized recruitment consultancy firm. After twenty-two years in the business, he decided it was time to retire. He had no choice but to sell the family assets to a rival firm for an undisclosed fee. Part of that deal ensured Steven, his oldest, would remain at the company as long as he wished.

Of course, Steven was extremely grateful. He enjoyed the job, and the travelling involved, seeking new clients or interviewing new candidates. Although he spent only a fraction of the time his father endured in this role, Steven was good at what he did. So good that he remembers the day he pulled in an important client. For the first time, his father told him he was incredibly proud of him. This cemented their already close relationship. He would never forget that day.

As he headed out of Castle Drum Park, he thought more about Ryan and convinced himself it would be a good idea if he visited him that afternoon. A surprise visit was the right thing to do. What would Ryan expect of him? Would Ryan want a visitor? There was only one way to find out, and that was to take the twenty-five-minute walk across town and surprise him.

Ryan might like that, he thought.

He had two choices. He could follow the long, winding road through town or take a shortcut through the narrow streets, including an area nicknamed *the jungle*. The concrete jungle was a dangerous and unpredictable place for unfamiliar faces, but not to Steven; he was known. People who weren't local tended to take the longer route to avoid confrontation with the natives.

Castle Drum was a place where unemployment was high, and poverty was rife. Drugs had been an enormous problem throughout the eighties and nineties. The estate once boasted forty-two thousand people in approximately ten square miles.

Old concrete buildings housed eight families. With so many people in such proximity; it created tensions. People felt they were living in each other's pockets constantly. Alcohol was a big issue with the youngsters and fights became pretty standard, especially at weekends when local teenagers fought over their territory. The area was small. You could drive through it in around six minutes, but the locals had split it into smaller sections, and only the brave would wander between sectors and into unfamiliar land. It was like war games on a minute scale. Knives and baseball bats were common. A joke circulated about the local sports shop. They often ran out of baseball bats, but were always fully stocked with baseballs and gloves.

He could see Ryan's house in the distance after taking the quick route. Most people went about their daily business. The teenagers were still in school except a few who had given up and sat in their gardens drinking cheap cider and listening to techno music blaring from the windows.

He knocked on the door of the first-floor flat. Ryan's girlfriend, still in her housecoat, answered within seconds.

'Ah! Steven, so nice to see you.'

Gemma welcomed him with open arms.

'Is he home?'

'Yes, he's in the kitchen. Go through.'

'How are you doing, brother?'

'What the fuck are you doing here?'

Ryan's enormous smile couldn't have been removed with a sheet of sandpaper.

'I was in the park reminiscing about old times and how things have changed. We've all grown up and become a lot wiser. Well, I have, can't say much about you, you thick cunt.' He winked and slapped Ryan on the back.

'Stay the fuck away from that place, Steven. It's bad news. I haven't been down there for a long time; I hate the place, scared of temptation, I suppose.'

'That's fantastic, bro. Looks like you're doing well here; you both seem happy.'

'We're doing just brilliant; I started work a few weeks back, I got myself a position as a forklift driver at the ANI Warehouse, it's a great wee job. Life's good, brother.'

Steven was relieved at the good news and stayed for a few hours. They drank tea and ate too many biscuits. Despite the hilarity, a serious side of their conversation emerged. It wasn't something Steven had expected.

During the conversation, Ryan thanked him and credited him with improving his life. He explained that, although he had ignored Steven's suggestions at the height of his habit, he hadn't forgotten the many attempts to help him. When Ryan decided it was time to attend a rehabilitation centre and create a better life, he had carried all Steven's words in his head. It helped him in such a way that he couldn't ever pay him back.

A tear ran down Steven's cheek when Ryan told him while he was going through his detox program he remembered the words of wisdom provided on cards by Steven. He would read them repeatedly each night. Sometimes he cried himself to sleep. He also wanted to rekindle the relationship they once had. Ryan had also written memories of what had made him happy during their childhood. It had been his way of passing the time in rehabilitation. Ryan couldn't praise his brother enough and was now a completely different man from the one Steven had met two months ago at their parents' home. Ryan had woken up and saw there was a lot more to life. He had more determination and confidence, much to Steven's satisfaction. After leaving Ryan, Steven felt nothing but relief, delight, and a slight sense of achievement.

What he thought was a waste of time had played a part in saving his brother. It had been over six months since he had last been in his brother's house. On that occasion, the house had been a shithole. A filthy kitchen and bathroom, the living room was dark, stuffy with a foul odour. Ryan had refused to open the curtains, never mind a window. This time around was different. The home was spotless; even the living room had a coat of paint and new blinds. Men can be clumsy in decoration and styles, so the woman's touch had done it for his brother.

Steven was delighted for Ryan and Gemma. After all their years of drug addiction, they now had a home they could be proud of. They had also adopted a continuous positive mindset necessary for their life's journey.

Feeling good about himself, he decided it was time for a pint. The nearest pub was not far away.

The sun's out for another few minutes at least, so I could do with a nice cold pint of cider with plenty of ice, Steven thought.

He looked at the dark clouds approaching in the distance. Even if it was only still ten degrees celsius, it was time for a walk to the pub.

'Imagine meeting you here!' Donna turned her petite figure around as Steven walked across the pub car park.

'Are you sure you're not fucking following me?' He laughed.

She tossed her long blonde hair to one side.

'Indeed, I am. I saw you earlier when I was on the bus. Were you visiting Ryan?'

'Yes, it was great to see him; he's finally turned things around for himself.'

Today she looked different. There was something on her mind. She seemed happy, and, as always, pretty stunning. He opened the door for her, then grabbed a seat next to the window, looking out over the car park. The trees were now moving as the wind rose and the sky darkened. Clouds were ready to open and soak the place. Although it was a miserable day outside, it was cosy inside. After a few more ciders, it was time for them to head back to his flat.

Steven was confused as far as Donna was concerned; she fucked with his head. He was fed up with always being friend-zoned and wanted more to their relationship than fuck buddies. He had had a crush on her for what seemed like an eternity. But progress was being made; their meetings becoming more frequent.

The following day, Steven was hungover. Donna had left the flat for a job interview by the time he woke up. A lazy day at home was required. He couldn't make work even if he wanted to. Thankfully, his unusual employment circumstances meant he could do what he wanted as part of a four-person team. Unknown to management, they struggled to find enough to keep them occupied, so taking the day off was not an issue. Even though he enjoyed the job, he had questioned himself over the last few months, wondering if this was how he saw his future. Maybe it was time for a change.

Sitting flicking through the TV channels, he found nothing of interest and browsed YouTube for something better.

There had been one date that changed Steven's outlook on the world, 11th September, 2001. Not because two towers were standing in downtown New York that morning and were gone in the afternoon, but he woke up to something else that had happened and couldn't let it go.

He pressed the play arrow on YouTube and watched the video he had already seen an exaggerated self-estimated three thousand times. So, he had a strong viewpoint, but it was not the attacks themselves that he had the issue with; it was the UK mainstream media.

While he watched the horrendous events unfold live, the BBC reported that world trade centre seven had collapsed, when indeed, the building was standing in all its glory over the reporter's shoulder. He remembered back to when he had sat with his nineteen-year-old friends. Around six of them had been in his bedroom, shouting at the TV in pantomime style. 'It's behind you!' Most of his friends joked about it, called the BBC amateurs, and laughed.

Only years later, Steven took an interest in the stories worldwide. What stories were important? What stories were not newsworthy? Why were stories of the public interest not covered by any of the UK media? He had previously heard all the stories from the older generations about the Poll Tax riots in Scotland and how the Scottish media failed to report on the issues that affected people. People's homes were emptied because of an unfair tax implemented by the Tories, but only in Scotland. The Scots were guinea pigs to Thatcher's Tory government.

Then, of course, there was the bullshit that The Sun newspaper reported on the Hillsborough disaster. Ninety-six Liverpool fans lost their lives during an FA cup semifinal match because of enormous crowds entering a stadium that was already full. Most people knew the agenda of this bastard newspaper, but occasionally, when some people were not aware, Steven wasn't slow at sharing the facts. The Scum, as it's known, reported that Liverpool fans urinated on the rescuers and robbed the dead. Steven would emphasise that it took The Sun fifteen years to apologise to the families involved. He hated the reporters with a passion.

Nowadays, he realised there was nothing he could have done in his late teenage years. Steven had been just one of the little people and didn't have the social media options he has available today. He enjoyed life back then with many friends and lots of girlfriends, but now he can count the people close to him on one hand. He's since become a bit of a loner and often uses the phrase Circles Small, Less Bullshit, which he stood by. Steven believed you don't need many people around you to be happy, just the right people.

With the need to find something else to pass the time, he picked up his laptop. Sitting on top was a note he hadn't noticed, even though he had walked past it a few times that morning. Love Donna, she had written at the bottom.

After reading the brief note, which all but confirmed he and Donna would be an item, he danced badly around his living room. He slid across the dark wooden flooring in his socks and boxer shorts and thought that all his patience and perseverance had paid off.

He grinned. Was he about to get what he had always wanted?

⊷⊶◅◈▻⊷⊶

Chapter 2

Seeking employment was more complicated than she imagined. She had a job, but it was only sixteen hours a week working behind the front desk of the only hotel in town. She headed off for her shift. Donna needed more hours. She struggled financially to keep her head above water. Her clothes were of the cheaper variety, but she looked classy no matter what she wore. Donna could wear a black bin liner and still draw attention from the lads. She budgeted for her meals and knew how to spread things out regarding food. The knowledge she gained as a chef's assistant in a local pub chain for a few years benefited her. The position had only been for the money. She hated the job and the management, but she never forgot the skills she gained.

She had recently celebrated her thirty-sixth birthday and looked back on her life. There was more to offer the world, but it never gave her a chance. She had been in many jobs, so far, she had found nothing enjoyable. Remembering her teenage years when her dream was to be a model, Julia Roberts sprung to mind. Now and again she watched Pretty Woman, without a doubt her most-watched movie ever. The happiness of the film also brought some unwanted memories.

'You'll never be a model,' a boy shouted across the playground of Castle Drum secondary school.

'You wait and see; when I'm older, that's how I'm going to make a fortune. You little prick!'

'You're too small; you got short legs.'

The boys burst out laughing.

Donna was unaware that being tall was a strict requirement to be a model and nothing like the slight frame that stood before her in the mirror. She spoke to her mum, who tried to convince her she still has a lot of growing to do at fourteen. However much Donna wanted to believe it, her mother didn't convince her.

One day, while looking in the mirror, she burst into tears when she realised her dreams would never become a reality. At five feet eight, it burst her bubble for the first time in her brief life. Small as she was, she took her gorgeous face from her mother. She wasn't short of attention with her slim body and long blonde hair.

Many people asked her about the possibility of her modelling later in life, as height became less of an issue with clothing companies. But, by that time, she had accepted that she has been born in the wrong generation and from the incorrect postcode.

Attractive as she was, it delighted her to be on her own. She had a few brief relationships over the years, but none lasted more than eleven months. She didn't see herself settling down with anyone soon. Donna had never been the party-goer or enjoyed the social scene of nightclubs that everyone else couldn't get enough of. She always opted for a night in front of the TV or a trip to the cinema before pubs and clubs. If she had a drink, it would be a few ciders at home and maybe the odd visit to a pub, but never a late night.

As she made her way to work on the bus, she saw her old friend, Steven. He looked to be walking through town, probably heading towards his brother's house.

I need to see him. She smiled.

Even though she had seen him the previous day, that wasn't enough. She enjoyed being around him. She knew she was safe in his company and that he was a friend she could trust. Donna had gone through every year of school with Steven, so their friendship stretched over thirty years.

I'll call him after work, she thought.

Minutes before she started her four-hour shift, there was a scream.

'Can someone help? Please help!'

A loud, panicked voice came from the hotel corridor.

Donna placed her coffee on top of the back office filing cabinet and hurried to see what the commotion was.

'My husband, he's stopped breathing!'

'Call an ambulance immediately,' Donna instructed another member of staff.

'Can you hear me, sir? Are you with us, sir?'

She checked for vital signs, carrying out the A, B and C checks; airways, breathing and circulation.

'Can everyone stand back, please? Get these people back!' her authoritative voice issuing instructions to the approaching manager.

Donna had completed a first aid course but had never put it into practice in a real-life situation.

There was no sign of life; the elderly gentleman wasn't breathing. She instinctively began CPR; the kiss of life, along with chest compression.

'Does anyone else know how to do this?' she yelled, aware that she might need help to continue the tiring procedure. 'Anyone?'

There was no response from the people standing a few feet away in the hotel lobby. It was then she realised she was on her own. At that moment, as if by some miracle, the man began breathing again. It only took two breaths and sixty chest compressions to get a response, much to her relief.

'Thank you! Thank you! God is watching over you.'

The voice came from his elderly wife, who stood with tears streaming down her cheeks. Donna placed the man in a recovery position and waited for six minutes until an ambulance arrived. These six minutes seemed like her entire four-hour shift.

'He's breathing now,' his wife explained to the paramedics.

While still in a state of panic, she pointed out the semi-unconscious man. It was at this point Donna realised what had happened. She had acted on impulse and thought nothing of it. As soon as the ambulance crew had the man stable, Donna left the lobby and went straight into the back office. It was there she just let go and broke down. The reality of the situation hit home. She knew she had saved someone's life, but she also realised how precious life is.

It was now twenty-five minutes past her starting time.

'Why don't you forget about working today?' her manager suggested.

'I can't afford to take time off.'

'Forget about the money. We'll just put it through for you. Take some time to get over what you've just done and the ordeal you've experienced. You're a hero to that old lady out there, and to us.'

'I need to be around people. Can I stay here in the office?'

'Of course, no problem at all. I'll put the kettle on.'

A couple of hours passed before Donna was back to her usual self. Folk at the hotel were there for her and made her feel much better, more than she would have felt if she had left, gone back home and been alone. Donna needed a drink—a pint of cider with plenty of ice.

'I'll meet up with Steven,' she announced to the others.

'Awe, Steven is lovely; he'll look after you alright.'

At least one colleague approved.

Donna headed to the pub with the sole intention of having one drink. Then she would give Steven a call. It was as she arrived at the pub car park she spied him. She had never thought about having a relationship with him, but today was different because of her afternoon ordeal and the realisation that time was precious. When he jokingly asked if she was following him, she remembered the conversation.

'Imagine meeting you here?'

'Are you sure you're not fucking following me?'

Steven laughed.

'Yes, I am, seen you earlier when I was on the bus; were you visiting Ryan?'

'Yes, it was great to see him; he's finally turned things around for himself.'

'I'm so glad to see you today; let's go inside for a much-needed pint, and I will tell you all about it. I'm a hero, allegedly!'

She smiled while looking him dead in the eyes.

They sat through a few more pints and then decided enough was enough. Steven had to work the next day, and Donna had a job interview.

'I'm staying at your place tonight.'

She looked at Steven with go to bed eyes that no man could refuse.

'You realise that I'm going to fuck you then?'

'What I'm going to do to you tonight will be like never before.'

She grabbed hold of him with both arms around his neck.

'I could get used to it. We could arrange that if you were my full-time girlfriend. I mean, you really should accept this offer now while it's on the table. There are so many other females queuing up for the opportunity to spend the rest of their lives with me.'

They burst out laughing, knowing there was no one else.

'Interesting opportunity. I might have to take you up on that.'

The talking ended once they stood in the middle of the road kissing, ignoring everything and everyone around them.

'Get a fucking room, you two!' the passenger in a white transit van shouted as the driver gave a few blasts of the horn.

But she felt different when they arrived at Steven's flat. Was she doing the right thing? What if it destroyed the most extended friendship either of them had had? What if something happened to one of them? What if the chance was gone forever without knowing what could have been? She had to take that chance.

Within minutes of entering the flat, they had ripped each other clothes off and headed straight for the bed. This differed from any previous sexual encounter they had shared. This time wasn't just a fuck; there was more intense passion than before. Even the foreplay lasted and the sex went on longer than usual. They fucked all over the bedroom in several positions, some positions they had never tried before.

Afterwards, they shared pillow talk, but neither wanted to sleep first. They lay cuddling and enjoying each other's company. Steven always wanted this, but Donna was the one who had the reservations. This time, both had the night of their lives, and they wanted more.

Donna woke up feeling fresh. She had only drunk one pint to Steven's two. She needed a shower and tried to creep around the room, leaving Steven sleeping. His shower was much better than hers and, because she often stayed over, her toiletries were already there. Under the steaming hot shower, she took time to think about their discussion the previous night. Donna enjoyed the night of passion and thought it was time for her to commit. She couldn't stop smiling. She knew her happiness was real and that she would make Steven thrilled after years of trying.

'He deserves to be happy. We both do,' she said out loud, even though she was alone in the bathroom.

Although she had some belongings at Steven's flat, she didn't have a fresh change of clothes, especially for a job interview. She needed to get home and pretty quickly. She wasn't aware if he had to be at his work early, so she didn't want to wake him but wanted to let him know how she felt. In the living room, she found a notebook and pen.

Good morning, my handsome man,

Thank you for last night; it was something extraordinary. I would indeed like to be your other half, but first, you need to take me out on an actual date, LOL.

If you ask, I will accept. I'm free tonight if you are.

I can't wait to see you.

Love Donna xxx.

She left Steven's flat, feeling the happiest she had been for a long time; there could be a real future between them. Normally, she told her friends she was unlucky in love. The men she attracted were not the ones she wanted anymore. The ones she didn't attract were the ones she should have chased. These men were often too afraid to speak to her, never mind make the first move.

She took public transport to the interview. For this role, she had minimal experience. The advert said an administrative assistant was required in a large company that sold computer components. Compared to what she was earning, the pay was good. Not so much the hourly rate, but the guaranteed thirty-five hours per week. She was nervous.

As she sat on the ninety-six bus, all she could think about was Steven and how she would walk down the aisle to marry him one day. Would Steven ever propose? Would they marry in a church? How would her dress look? In a moment of happiness, she daydreamed of the perfect wedding, which made the journey time fly past.

Donna's younger sister, Lynda, was a party animal. On most occasions, her nights out continued until the following day. Three years before, Lynda had married a guy Donna had never liked. But they had the dream wedding, only for it to fall to pieces after fourteen months. Lynda had a thing for bad boys, and with bad boys, there are issues and consequences. They might drive the latest Audi funded by their drug trade, but the threat of other nice-looking women out there wanting the same lifestyle made it almost impossible for Donna's ex-brother-in-law to keep his dick in his trousers. These thoughts made her want to settle with Steven, as he was nothing like her sister's type of guy.

Donna left the office building and the interview behind her.

Thank fuck that's over.

'How do you think it went?' Steven asked when he called later that day.

'The interviewer was an awkward bitch; I have no chance of getting it,' she replied, with a hint of disappointment in her voice.

'Look, Donna, you have me now, so worry less. You are not alone anymore.'

He wanted to make her feel better.

'Thanks, honey.'

'Just come over, and I'll make you dinner tonight. I've just arrived at work, but I'll be home in a few hours. Your favourite, Lasagne. OK?'

Four days passed, and again Donna was feeling the financial pinch as she headed to her work for a meagre four hours. If the job gave her more hours, she would be happy and look forward to going in each day. Donna blamed the government for allowing such zero-hour contracts to happen. She hadn't been interested in politics, but now she was older and wiser, her curiosity grew.

As she entered the hotel, she spotted her manager, Christine, chatting to an elderly couple; all she could see of them were their backs. Donna noticed a massive bunch of flowers over the man's shoulders.

'There she is now.'

Christine pointed to the main door.

The couple turned around. Instantly, Donna recognised them. It was the elderly gentleman whose life she had saved and his wife.

'We thank you without the previous hysteria,' joked his wife.

'You don't know how much this means to my family; we can't thank you enough.'

The man smiled as he handed the bouquet to Donna.

'They're beautiful! Thank you so much. You didn't have to. I never thought in a million years I would have to carry out my first aid training, although that experience makes it all worthwhile.'

Donna stifled her tears.

'We're expecting our first great-granddaughter any day now, and we are both so excited; if it weren't for your quick thinking, my husband would never meet her.'

'We just wanted to thank you in person. I've been to the hospital. Without going into great depressing details, they worked their magic, and here I am.' The man held his arms out. 'We have another gift for you. Please accept. We've thought this though, long and hard, and it would mean the world to us if you would accept.'

He handed Donna an envelope.

'What's this?'

She slowly opened the envelope.

'Just a little something as a real thank you. We both agreed that flowers don't quite cut it as payback, as nice as they are. There's three thousand pounds in there, tax-free, of course, unless you're stupid enough to declare it.'

The woman patted her on the shoulder with a wink and a smile.

A puddle of tears welled in Donna's eyes as she looked at the money. She began shaking.

'But I only did what anyone else would have done; it was the right thing.'

'But no one else was here that day, my dear. It was only you.'

'I'm going to cry soon, maybe in the next three seconds!'

She half laughed as she let her tears flow.

'These are tears of happiness; you don't know how much this means to me. I'm in a tricky financial situation right now, and you would never believe how much you have helped me. I really can't thank you enough.'

Donna was about to wipe her tears with her sleeve when her manager handed her a tissue and offered them tea and a light snack. He told Donna to join them in the lounge. They spent the next forty minutes chatting about life and how precious a gift it was. The couple shared experiences of their lives and impressed Donna when they admitted to being married for fifty-one years.

The experience taught Donna that there could be lasting love out there; if she looked hard enough, maybe it had been right in front of her nose all along.

Chapter 3

People are dying.

Not just in third world countries, but across the globe in nations considered world leaders in global finance, science and technology. The natives are getting restless. Can this go on for much longer?

Will the people rise?

If this is the world we live in, can we ensure that all elections are honest and fair?

Why would the people vote for such austerity and misery?

Is it because it's the best of a bad bunch?

Has the political system failed the people?

Why do political parties get away with U-turning on manifesto pledges without consequence?

Scandals make the nation's newspapers for a day, then people simply forget them. They vanish like they never happened. Swept under the carpet. Can the power of social media and the internet change the world before it gets disconnected from itself?

There are many questions to be asked, Steven thought late one Monday night before closing his laptop and making the slow, sleepy walk from the sofa to the bedroom.

A typical Tuesday morning dawned. Although the sun was shining on the front garden, the rain had soaked the back garden. This was nothing unusual for the UK, even at the peak of summer. Steven sat up in bed, his dog staring him in the eye with a kind of 'you're late' look. It needed out. At twenty-seven minutes after the first of his daily walks, they were late.

After a quick wash, Steven donned his stylish green jacket that wouldn't look out of place in an Oasis music video. It was time he walked the dog across the local fields without forgetting his doggy poo bags. Even taking the dog for a walk without these small toilet bags could result in a fine of several twenty-pound notes if you have bad luck and the chance of meeting any plastic community police officers. They are the type who wanted to join the force but were too fucking stupid, too fucking fat or couldn't join because they had debt. They felt just as important, but on a smaller salary. The type of fuckers who were bullied at school and wanted to feel a specific power of revenge on society.

As Steven set foot out the door, he heard some unusual commotion in his ordinarily quiet residential area for that time in the morning; voices and car engines running. As he got closer to the scene, he saw several police cars, an ambulance, and a private ambulance were present. He saw Linda, someone he had known since he was a teenager. They were from the same estate. He realised she was working, only there to pick up a body and nothing more. Very professional, one of a kind and down to earth, just like Steven. Once he witnessed her daily routine close up, things changed. He gained much more respect for her.

Then he noticed Fiona. She shook in her pyjamas while smoking a cigarette. With her hair all over the place, she looked on edge.

'What's happened, Fiona?'

'It's old Stanley; it seems they've just discovered his body this morning, and he's been dead for about two days. Steven, it's just tragic.'

Fiona took another draw of her cigarette with her shaking hand.

Steven stood silently. Fiona's eyes were red and her face puffy.

'I know how this has happened; it's the government's fault!' she shouted in a rage to make sure the emergency services heard her cries.

It did little good. These services also felt the cutbacks of a cruel, austerity-driven government.

'Can I have a word, please, madam?' An officer approached Fiona. 'Did you know the deceased?'

'Yes, I knew him very well; it's all the government's fault, they're lying, cheating, robbing bastards, all of them. He was fighting for his pension and had gone without money for almost nine weeks. I spoke to him on Sunday, and he was at an all-time low. He didn't have any food or heating; I had to help him out with what little I could spare.'

She burst into tears.

This angered Steven, but there was nobody there to listen. He felt there was no point in further upsetting Fiona or risking arrest by shouting his head off. He could have faced a breach of the peace charge, something they can arrest you for in the UK. This includes using foul language in public, which is a fucking joke. He needed to take the dog for a walk and think of how this would have made national headlines in a hypothetical situation.

Pensioner starved to death by those he voted into power.

An excellent headline choice, but there's more chance of the dog pooping in his own bag and putting it in the bin himself, thought Steven.

He arrived back at his flat pretty fucking angry. Only the night before, after he logged on to his usual Anonymous forum, he read similar stories about people dying in Italy and France from austerity measures. Whether it was true was another story. Steven didn't believe it was the gospel from random people posting online. Still, he thought about how many people would genuinely feel about his story after reading what he had just experienced.

He didn't surf the internet like most of the population; he was involved in the darker side of the internet. It's what's known as The Onion browser. On the dark side, Anonymous groups were the most common. Hackers and experts all trying to outdo each other by taking over corporate computer systems. They carried out DOS attacks to cripple websites. DOS is an abbreviation of 'Denial of Service'. Literally, people use specialist software to make the website think that thousands of people are trying to access simultaneously. The website host server can't handle the traffic, so it crashes, making it inaccessible for legit customers. If as little as ten people used this software simultaneously, it would take down even the most prominent companies.

This was where Steven thought about old Stanley. What if he could find someone, tell them his story, and take down the UK's Department of Work and Pensions website?

Was it possible to take over the website completely?

Maybe place a picture of Stanley with some kind of message.

You have Blood on your Hands, sounded right.

It was time to find someone with the capabilities, as something like this was totally out of Steven's league. To him, this was the champions' league geek level.

Seven hours after he posted Stanley's story, Steven received a private encrypted message from someone who held a humongous reputation around the underground internet known as Midnight Justice. The moniker was taken because anytime he had carried out previous attacks; it was always midnight in the country he attacked.

Not the most thought-through nickname for someone so intelligent, Steven thought.

Steven suggested his idea to Midnight. He responded by laughing hysterically, sending twenty laughing emojis.

'We are going much more significant than posting a picture or taking down the DWP website. Things will happen on a national scale soon,' Midnight replied as he posted a link to a private group that only the invited could access.

The group had similar security to what WhatsApp had implemented. It's so heavily encrypted, even the FBI couldn't access messages involved in murder cases.

Nobody owned this group; nobody outside the group had any knowledge of its existence, as they were all sworn to secrecy. Everyone in the group had as much to lose as the next man, so they trusted each other. Steven read some posts. Some dated back to two years ago when they set up the group. He was in disbelief at what he read. Some ideas were so far-fetched they would make Die Hard movies look like Disney. Some were just outright terrorism. Others wanted justice on a smaller scale, with nobody getting hurt or dying, which appealed to Steven.

The one thing most people agreed on was that politicians were eventually to be the targets. The ruling elite, the liars, the ones who sleep on the job with no consequences. The ones who backtrack on policies after getting into power on the back of lies. Corruption and expenses scandals were a massive topic. Regular people saw politicians taking advantage of the system they put in place.

If the average person or woman on the street gets caught fiddling expenses at their workplace, they are sacked and go back to the job centre. That's it in a nutshell. Politicians apologise, pay it back, say it's a genuine error, and carry on doing the job. You couldn't have made this shit up.

Excitement took over, and his adrenalin was pumping. Steven was like a dog with two cocks. With a spring in his step, he made his way to the kitchen for something to remove the hunger until it was teatime. He looked at the clock, then realised it was almost nine o'clock. He scratched his head and wondered where the time had gone. Had he really been sitting on his Mac for the last six hours, engrossed in all the plans people had for the government?

It wasn't just the government; others were to be held accountable. Others were just as guilty as the government in people's eyes, and this was to be happening sooner than he imagined. Thanks to a member's idea and simplicity, the mainstream media were now the first targets.

The standard position amongst most of the groups was that the UK mainstream media ignored most things that governments wanted hidden. After all, Rupert Murdoch and the likes fund political parties. Then there's the BBC, an upper class, leftist, liberal mouthpiece, which is state-owned, but really doesn't give a fuck, and reports what it wants with no form of consequences. This includes pushing its political correctness and immigration agenda. A publicly funded corporation with so many upper class, out-of-touch people running the show. Then there's SKY, who make their own agenda and ignore most daily stories that affect the working class. They are all partly responsible, and the people don't forget.

The plan was a straightforward, simple vandalism attack. An army of people who would simultaneously set fire to cars in as many media source car parks as possible, from the newspapers to the giant corporations of our screens. There were specific rules, though. You must target the mainstream media HQ closest to your home if you take part. If there were underground car parks in any of the locations, they were to be left alone; this would minimise the chance of people getting trapped. Only cars parked outside the building were worthy of some lighter fuel and a match thrown through a broken window.

The site informed everyone that if they smashed an old spark plug into small pieces and then used the white glass, it would quietly break the car window with ease. Others opted to steal the emergency plastic hammers from buses. Genius thinking, but at a danger to the public and expense to the bus companies, but they didn't really give a fuck. It was a small price, and it's not as though people used these hammers daily on buses across the country.

Steven felt lucky. He lived twenty minutes by bus from BBC London; almost a straight road all the way. He agreed to meet with another eight people. They took individual walks and did some research on the building and car parks, noting what days were the busiest. Steven was to visit the area the following day.

With his regular oversized green overcoat, flowerpot hat and wearing sunglasses, he rolled up to the car park in a clever disguise. One that security footage trying to identify him at a later date would not find sufficient in court should things go wrong. Cars packed the car park and no security personnel attended the flimsy barrier. It was Thursday afternoon at a quarter past two exactly.

Steven went back on the forum and, between them, they established that Mondays or Thursdays were the days of the week when the car park was at its busiest, almost to capacity. Not at all locations, but the majority were also active on these days. People wanting easy Fridays could have been the reason for busy Thursdays.

By the small hours of the morning, the majority had decided that Thursday would be the time of the attack. The groups printed their own messages, which were to be left lying across the car park's ground on their exit.

Standard A4 size paper, with various notes, which read;

Lying Bastards.

UK Mainstream Media–Assisting the establishment to hide the truth. DWP has blood on their hands.

Tell the Truth.

Report Real Stories.

Power to the people.

Government Puppets.

Some also included the name of a famous female reporter, who they alleged had sucked cock all the way to the top job. Nothing threatening, just what each member felt like getting off their chest.

The following Thursday, Steven was nervous but excited. He took a few minutes to justify his actions later that afternoon. Would the media cover it? Would they really cover up an attack on themselves? Would they be doing this for nothing? He thought for a minute that he was doing this not just for Stanley, but for many other reasons.

The bedroom tax was one issue that really affected several of his friends. It was disgusting, and he often compared it to the ancient window tax, as it was known. King William the third, introduced the Sunlight Tax in 1699; it lasted one hundred and fifty years. The more windows you had in your home, the higher the tax. The bedroom tax was very similar, as most bedrooms had a window. Imagine a world where you are taxed on fucking sunlight? It was similar, no matter how they dressed it up and forced the people to accept it.

One woman was being charged extra because her son left home to travel for a year before going back to university. The single mother had done the honourable thing and informed the local council he was leaving, which resulted in her having additional costs that she could not afford. Only because the son was sending money back every few months she could stay in the house where she had lived for twenty-four years. This was more motivation that added to the reasons he already had.

Dressed, as usual, Steven took the bus through the busy Market Street. It was almost a straight road, with sandstone tenement buildings the entire street length and a variety of shops underneath. A bustling street, which could turn the usual journey into thirty minutes, but that gave him more thinking time.

Carrying the bag with his disguise, he met up with the rest of the team. Some were armed with broken white spark plug glass and others with small glass shattering hammers, stolen from various buses across the city. They also had lighter fuel poured into plastic energy drink bottles to make it easier to flow through the drinking nozzles. It wasn't ideal trying to get liquid from a small lighter fuel can with a tiny pinhole when you're in a hurry; that was too time-consuming. Their time to shine has arrived.

They sneaked into the car park where at least thirty, possibly forty cars, in groups of three were parked. One group took the furthest away cars, while the others started in the middle. Not every vehicle was to be targeted. They had discussed previously that if two vehicles were on fire at either side, the car in the middle would eventually catch fire. It was enough to smash the back or side windows. This would be the quickest way to make the fuel tank catch fire.

Nine people, three teams of three. The first one breaks the window, the second person pours in the lighter fuel, and the third person throws in the match. Standing in position at cars number one, three and five, in went the first window. Not the quietest smash they hoped for, but not loud enough to let any by passers know what was happening. Things would already be in full swing before realisation came to anyone.

The first car went up in flames in an instant. They went over the score with the fuel. Within twenty seconds, three cars were ablaze with smoke that would attract attention in minutes. This went too easy, though. Something had to give. Almost three minutes had passed and, in the BBC London car park, two-thirds of the cars were bursting with flames. It was only a matter of time before the other third caught on.

The groups ran for the gate and the barrier. The team noticed a security guard; he walked towards them and spoke into his radio. Obviously, he requested help from the emergency services. As he got closer, Steven had to decide. Nobody was to get caught, and nobody was to be hurt, but this jobsworth security officer on the minimum wage was getting in the way. They carried out these actions for people like him, but it's not as though Steven had time to stop and explain. He used some scare tactics to ensure the security guard backed off. He went into his pocket and threw all the bits of paper in the air. There was such a rush of adrenalin going through their minds; the others forgot this was part of the plan.

As soon as Steven did this, the rest followed. The security guard looked somewhat confused at nine men and women throwing bits of paper into the air like confetti, and he stood still. One of the team shouted to the guard.

'You have a family! I have petrol and matches. We are running out of here, and you will go home to them tonight.'

The guard ran backwards, talking on his radio.

'We've done it! Run!' Gary shouted.

They ran far enough away and then calmed down into a slow jog; Steven and another four took a back street where there were no cameras. He stripped off the disguise, as did the others. They stuffed the items in a bin, set the waste container alight, and went their separate ways.

Steven heard the sirens. He could also smell the smoke, it was everywhere. People could see a massive cloud of smoke in the sky for miles. With curiosity getting the better of him, he returned to the scene of the crime. He wanted to see the damage first-hand.

'It could be a terrorist attack,' he heard one woman saying.

It was then he stopped to think. They describe a terrorist attack as an act of terror. The aim is to accomplish political gain. Was he a terrorist? Were our politicians terrorists? What was the difference here? The group had ensured nobody was injured; thousands of people died because of government policy. He justified his actions repeatedly because he was in the right; they all were. The people were not terrorists. they were now fighting for the people. The hierarchy had failed in so many ways. The realisation mixed with confusion made him feel something he had never experienced.

Arriving home shortly afterwards, Steven went straight to the fridge and pulled out a cold can of cider. He placed some ice in a glass and poured the strawberry and lime cider over the top. He went to the TV and switched on Sky News.

It was there, live on TV. He changed channels; it was on almost every news channel. Terrorists attack BBC London, Sky News HQ London, most UK tabloid newspapers HQ including The Sun, Daily Mail and Express, BBC Manchester, BBC Glasgow, BBC Wales, BBC Bristol, BBC Liverpool, BBC Dundee, BBC Bangor. Fifty-four BBC car parks were ablaze. This was global news.

Channel hopping from CBS News to CNN, both in the USA and then back to the UK mainstream media, he noticed one vast difference. No UK media outlet was reporting on the notes that littered every one of their car parks. It was as though it didn't happen. Only a few hours later, because of the power of social media, the UK mainstream media had to surrender and admit this was a UK people's power incident. It had nothing to do with Islamic extremists or any right-wing group. It was an enormous relief to see all the topics discussed globally. Why are people dying of starvation in the UK in the twenty-first century? Why were pensioners freezing to death after paying taxes their whole lives? The UK media even began questioning their own responsibility. This was a victory with something as simple as setting fire to cars with not one person injured. TV Channels eventually started guessing figures, with an estimate that they had damaged over three thousand cars, and ninety percent directly related to media employees. They had caused about one hundred and ten million pounds worth of damage.

Just as Steven started celebrating with his dog, another cider and, of course, the others in the anonymous forum, the bubble burst; breaking news on Sky. Steven almost dropped his cider. *Anonymous group threaten lives of journalists* flashed across the ticker at the bottom of the screen. This could not be happening, thought Steven in pure disbelief. This wasn't in the planning or even discussed.

Who the fuck did this? he asked himself.

Public opinion was on their side. People understood why this happened, but this would have damaged any public support, as threatening lives was in another league.

A few minutes later, BBC News was the first to report that the Glasgow group had left several notes. One particular message that was the most damaging stated, 'Change media policy. We know where you live.' That was a disaster.

Those mental fucking Jocks, thought Steven.

Two days passed, and Steven never left his Mac, never mind the house. Not the exact way he had planned his two-week holiday from work. He even let the dog out in the back garden on his own. His source of food came from fast food shops via home deliveries. His regular grocery and alcohol shopping came from Asda online, which was only just under a mile away. Nights turned into days, and panic took over. He constantly checked that his VPN was working one hundred percent. A VPN, the Virtual Private Network that tricked the internet into thinking the end-user was in a different country to where they were actually located. Steven always had his set to The Netherlands or Austria, as they were more relaxed than other European countries.

The chat in the forum was calm. Most people accepted that what was done was done, and they needed to move on, learn from it and try to repair the threats and win public opinion back. It was decided that Midnight Justice would release a video and explain that the threats were that of a lone wolf and had nothing to do with the group. The message sent to the world said, in the typical anonymous voice,

On Thursday, the United Kingdom's media saw the full wrath and capabilities of people's power. These are the consequences of your lies and failure to report the truth. Many politicians are guilty of fraud, extortion, drug abuse, child abuse, theft, neglect of duty, expenses scandals, amongst other things, while you, the media, failed to report them consistently. You are a one-sided, controlled organisation that cannot report genuine stories.

People across the United Kingdom are dead from starvation or have frozen to death in their homes and on the streets, yet you find this un-newsworthy. Shame on each and every one of you.

Our once great nation gave millions to countries that gave us absolutely nothing in return. Why do we give money to countries like Pakistan, which financed a nuclear weapons programme?

Why did we give India, who are another nuclear weapons nation, one billion pounds? When they spent three hundred and thirty million on a statue? Why are we giving over three hundred million to the likes of Nigeria, which has one of the most corrupt governments on the planet? How could anyone justify giving away over thirteen billion in total when we have ex-servicemen sleeping on our own streets? Do we have a housing crisis? Of course we do.

Over one million children live in direct poverty, with some getting their only meal of the day at school. Nothing can convince the British people that this is the right way to spend our taxable income.

We, Anonymous, claim full responsibility for setting fire to as many media staff cars as possible, but we wish to make things clear that at no point did we put any lives in danger. The Glasgow notes were not in our plans and were the actions of a lone wolf who left his own opinions. We do not tolerate the threatening of lives. We have other methods to grab your attention and cause disruption to companies and individuals.

We are anonymous. We are legion. We do not forgive. We do not forget.

Expect us'.

Chapter 4

A few days went by, and MPs were disgusted, calling the attacks nationalist terrorism.

Are you fucking serious? thought Steven.

People were dying, kids were starving, hundreds of thousands were living on the streets, and the Prime Minister and his cronies refused to listen.

What exactly did they expect? A pat on the back and tell them not to worry, we'll survive?

We know you have a tough job. We're cold and hungry, but we'll get there in the end. All this while politicians rent out their London homes for a fortune, rent a second home and claim it on expenses. It really is a sick world that we live in. They designed the system this way; it's not by accident.

Protests took place outside Westminster daily, just like the protests we saw in the build-up to Brexit. People were getting restless and more furious. For once, the media started talking to real people outside the well-off areas, even going into some housing estates, schemes, as they are called in Scotland. This was so far from their usual agenda.

Have these actions worked as intended? Steven asked himself.

In normal circumstances, the media would look for the z-list celebrity who speaks up for the people, but not this time. Several times a day, the people watched interviews with regular angry working-class people. The people had got their voices back with media support, and MPs were being slaughtered for various reasons on many TV channels.

Morning and afternoon talk shows were becoming so popular. People were even watching them on catch-up TV after work. '

This is how it should be, Steven thought.

But would this continue, or would it just be like any other political scandal that is eventually swept under the carpet and fades out when the next big story arrives? Only time would tell.

It's time to take the dog out for a walk before bedtime, thought a half-drunk Steven.

He had managed an average of four hours of sleep each night over the last six days. It eventually caught up with him. Just as he went to get the dog's lead, he heard Breaking News on Sky by the stunning-looking, blonde female presenter.

'Two people have been injured in a mass arson attack across The Netherlands,' she said. 'Sky News understands that several media outlets across The Netherlands have been firebombed simultaneously, tonight around ten pm Central European Time, nine pm Greenwich Mean Time. It's thought the people injured were cleaners in the building.

A total of sixteen buildings have been attacked, all part of the Dutch mainstream media. We'll have more on this developing story as we get it.'

Steven immediately sat back down on his white leather sofa, ignoring an excited dog who thought it was his time to sniff some lamp posts. Reaching for his phone, he called Donna.

Steven and Donna had now developed a close relationship; she shared the same political opinions. They were also in agreement that the UK Government had screwed British society.

'Are you watching TV?' he asked.

'No, I'm on my way back from Asda; I had to get milk for the morning coffee,' she replied.

Her relieved voice implied she'd be OK at sunrise for her caffeine fix.

'Pop into my place on the way home; you really need to see what's on TV!' Steven sounded excited.

Ben got impatient. It was time for that walk. He headed in the direction he knew Donna was coming from and met her halfway. It was more of a light jog than a walk. The excitement was too much, and he almost skipped down the street at the news and the thought of seeing Donna again. She didn't expect to bump into him.

'Hey, Ben.'

She bent down and petted the dog.

'You'll never guess what's happened in Amsterdam; it's incredible,'

'Hello to you too.'

'I was going to say hello, but you acknowledged Ben first,' Steven joked.

As they walked back to the flat, Steven updated Donna on everything he had seen on the news channels and was eager to get back for more. It was like a drug to him. He needed more information, and right now, not when Sky decided. Donna filled the kettle while Steven put the TV on. He went straight to the menu of news channels.

He didn't have the usual TV system; he had IPTV (Internet Protocol Television), which enabled him to watch TV from all over Europe, even the Dutch channels he desperately wanted to view. Neither couldn't understand Dutch, but they got enough from the images to tell the story. Well, at least until Donna demanded he change it to something where they could get the entire story, or at least the media's version of the story.

The TV was repeating the last hour's news. They had no further updates. Although he asked Donna to come over, he felt it wouldn't be right to get his MacBook out and go online for genuine updates. He thought it would be anti-social, and it was not in his character to ignore guests, even if they were really close. The only way to get fresh updates was to get back online; the wait was making him edgy.

'Why don't you get some updates online, Steven?'

She got up to make more tea. With a quick nod of the head from Steven in agreement for another brew, he sprung off the sofa and grabbed his laptop.

'You're right; we'll get more from there than any media channels. Let's have a look together when the tea is ready,' he suggested.

Donna had removed any guilt about anti-social behaviour.

Steven logged in and ensured all his security was up to date and that his VPN was connected. Things had got serious, and the last thing he wanted was a knock on the door at six in the morning with the local constabulary connecting him with any of the UK attacks. He was ready, though. VPN connected to Austria, which was good enough.

As he connected to the forum, he noticed one post had over three thousand replies over the last hour. *Missing Dutch Journalist*, was the headline. He clicked it open and tried to get through the comments as fast as possible, but the forum was on fire. Post after post, he struggled to keep up and couldn't find the time to reply. Donna sat, saying nothing. They were reticent, watching with the TV volume at a minimum. The rain battered off the windows of the flat. After catching up with all the posts, they looked at each other.

'This has gone further than anyone could have imagined, Steven.'

He sensed fear in her voice.

'The Dutch are crazier than us Brits; it won't get as bad as that here in the UK.'

He tried to reassure her.

In the Netherlands, Anonymous had kidnapped a senior Dutch journalist, and he had not been heard of since the fire attack. The only reason the authorities were aware of his situation was because of the notes left behind.

We have Bert Koster in custody–Expect us–Anonymous.

Someone had written the words on cards then dumped them near to where his office car park was firebombed.

They planned this from the start. If it's not the Jocks, it's them crazy Dutch bastards. Steven's thoughts swirled.

The following morning, Donna had the milk for the coffee. She never made it home. She stayed at Steven's, something she did more often these days. Just as well she brought her own milk, because they had used all of Steven's when they sat up till after four in the morning, drinking tea while reading and listening to the news. The last rumours they heard was that Bert, the journalist, was safe and an update from Anonymous would be released in due course.

Around eleven that morning, Greenwich Mean Time, an announcement was expected. Ninety minutes to go. They had slept until nine-thirty that morning. Feeling tired, Steven realised Ben was well overdue for his walk and needs. Donna put the coffee on while he walked the pissed off, desperate dog. He took it a bit off track from the usual route as his intense thoughts pervaded. He got a little paranoid. It was insane, and through the actions of himself and others, things had spread to another country. Now they had kidnapped someone.

He thought about it and smiled. He shouldn't be paranoid, he should be proud of what he had done; as long as that journalist was fine and nobody else died, then everything was OK. He justified this to himself many times on the longer route home with Ben.

Politicians sent kid soldiers into illegal wars to die and got away with it. He had only joined this small group where there had been two attacks and kidnapping, which, for the latter, he convinced himself it involved an umbrella group. There had only been two minor injuries.

On his return to the flat, his coffee was cold; Donna had done some basic housework and had already showered. It was ten fifty-four exactly when a post titled I'm Sorry; They Made Me Do It showed up on the forum.

Donna had control of the laptop, even though Steven had returned from his dog walking.

There was a link to an MP4 file named *My Apology*.

'Quick! Download that before it's removed.'

But Donna had already begun the download. With the high-speed connection, it was with them immediately.

They looked at each other. There were hundreds of replies within minutes. Most people were still in the dark, but with an idea that this was a video of Bert Koster, one of the Netherlands' most popular media mules.

Nobody expected what was to come. Donna clicked on the play button.

Bert sat at an office desk with an Anonymous banner and a picture of their adopted Guy Fawkes masks. Behind him was their slogan.

We are anonymous. We are legion.

We do not forgive. We do not forget.

Expect us.

Bert certainly didn't expect them, that's for sure. It was less than twenty-four hours after the kidnapping, fourteen hours to be exact. He looked in good health, but nervous. His left hand shook as he held some papers. He had two members of Anonymous on either side of him wearing their masks and dressed in black boots, black trousers and black hoodies, with *Expect us* blazoned across the front in large red text.

Although Bert was a common household name in his homeland, he wasn't well known in other countries. This was his fifteen minutes of fame to shine on a global stage. A day and event he would never forget.

He spoke through the silence of Steven and Donna.

'To begin, I would like to inform my family, my employers and the police that I'm in excellent health and at no point was I ever in any danger. I'm feeling good and will be home to my wife, children and grandchildren in the next hour.'

The purpose of this act of kidnapping has been explained to me in great detail. For the good of society, I have to accept that I have been partly responsible for bias reporting and fake stories broadcast into the four million homes across the Netherlands. Your government has been paying TV companies for decades to report whatever they wish.

Sometimes it will be to raise social tensions, which will enable them to bring in new laws that will control you. Few people are aware of this, but hate crime was introduced to make things easier to destroy your freedom of speech. To silence the public.

After spending a short time with my kidnappers, I conclude that they have valid points.

For the good of society, it is totally unacceptable for us to continue the way we have for many decades. Humanity deserves better, and for that reason, I can't keep the same opinions and thought processes I have held for the last thirty-seven years as a professional journalist.

This was not just a wake-up call for me, but also for the public.

I hope you, the public, will forgive me and start challenging your governments and hold them accountable.

People vote for political parties on the grounds of their manifesto. After they are elected, U-turns on policy become more like daily business and no one bats an eyelid. Journalism ignores such drastic changes and, on most occasions, reports something that the public will be in outrage about. In contrast, MPs in most countries push things through parliament under the darkness of public distraction.

I will end this speech with a strange thank you to my kidnappers for handling the situation. I really think I have Stockholm syndrome. The cleverness they used to set me up and get me to play along with them, which I will not disclose, was remarkable. Under these circumstances, it would best that I resign not just from my position in various media, TV and tabloids, but from journalism in full.

I wish to assure my previous employers and government officials that I have met with and discussed important issues over the years; I have no intention of continuing as a whistle-blower or plan to write a book that would share the valuable information placed in my trust.

With everything said, they will release me from a secret location and reunite me with my family for some rest. I will comply with any ongoing police enquiry into my kidnapping and conduct a one-time interview for TV before I take a break for the foreseeable future. Thank you for your understanding.'

Steven and Donna sat speechless. They scrolled through comments, pointing at words and nodding their heads in agreement. The thought of what had happened and his involvement had stemmed from the death of Stanley. As they looked online, there was a massive celebration going on all over the world. Members were sharing a drink and posting their glasses of alcohol, no matter what time it was in their geographical location. That was when Steven went to the fridge and grabbed two bottles of Corona.

'Sorry, I've run out of lemon and lime!'

Donna took the cold bottle with one hand and pushed the laptop across the couch out of harm's way. She placed her thumb over the bottle and shook it like it was a small bottle of champagne, and let it explode over Steven's face.

'Woo hoo! Let's celebrate this occasion; these things don't happen every day, you know.' A soaked Steven burst out laughing with her.

He grabbed hold of her, placed his bottle on the table, and pulled her closer for a kiss.

'This is amazing, Steven.'

'Yes, I know I'm a good kisser.'

'Not the kissing, you idiot. How things are working out. It's a great feeling, it's changing things.'

'It's a great feeling, but not as great as having you here most of the time; why don't you move in with me?' Steven whispered in her ear.

Donna remained silent in thought, but hugged him tight. They were both thinking about how long it would take for the story to make the UK mainstream media. Since there was very little news of the kidnapping in the first place, they didn't expect the story to be followed up when Bert was released.

'Let's play Sky News bingo,' Donna said in a pretend game show host type voice, then laughed. 'Let's both pick times, and whoever gets the time that the breaking news occurs is the winner, and the loser needs to do a forfeit.'

As it was only them, they had to pick a few hours each to be a winner. They carried on until midnight.

The following day, they needed out of the flat. With the housework done, it was almost time for a late lunch. Having only drunk coffee, the hunger gripped. Lunch and a pint of cider sounded the perfect way for some relaxation. He suggested they visit The Fox Bar.

It was on the far side of Castle Drum was a nice little bar. It was dazzling because of the wall of windows facing towards the riverside. Old looking inside, it had a slight touch of modern, just enough not to remove the vintage look. Several stools took up space along the bar, oak tables and chairs scattered around the sides, with a few in the middle, next to the gambling machines. With an open fire as the centrepiece and a collection of old photos of Castle Drum on the wall around the fireplace, the bar welcomed its clients. It was quiet. It didn't have music and, although there were televisions on the walls, the sound was usually turned down. There were subtitles to give the regular solo drinkers something to focus on.

Donna loved the ten-minute journey on the train, and it dropped them off outside the pub; much better than the slower but cheaper bus. The riverside trip was as enjoyable as the delicious lunch and a pint.

As they walked into the bar, they noticed the huge televisions had the sound raised to a decent level for a change, no doubt at a customer's request. There were more people than usual paying attention. It was more like a scene from an American movie where everyone watched and stared into shop windows with tremendous interest. An MP was on the air.

The customers were quiet until one local pensioner shouted, 'These bastards need to get back to the real world!'

The message unfolding across the bottom of the screen was exactly what they were waiting for. *Kidnapped Dutch Journalist Bert Koster released unharmed.*

'I won the bingo!'

Donna prodded him while a grin stretched across her face.

Steven ignored her. He was motionless, speechless, and didn't know how to react. Donna missed the ticker across the screen, but it took complete hold of Steven. *Anonymous urges European citizens to monitor their local journalists' and politicians' actions continuously and hold them accountable regularly.*

Donna ordered two pints of dark fruit cider and pointed to some seating nearer the television.

'This is getting out of control, Donna. I can't deal with the scale of this anymore,' Steven whispered.

He felt the pressure for the first time. He was paranoid about his connection with the underground group that kicked things off. It was taking its toll. He picked up his cider and took a few gulps, taking the contents to under half.

As if things couldn't get any worse, Sky confirmed that Anonymous had released a statement and they would return after the commercial break with further details. The television cut to the adverts and the noise in the bar increased dramatically; evidence that people had been listening.

The first commercial appeared on TV. Steven didn't notice the product; he could hear the soundtrack. Sum 41– In Too Deep. He listened to the lyrics.

Cause I'm in too deep, and I'm trying to keep up above my head, instead of going under.

They turned to each other. No words were spoken, but they dissolved into fits of laughter. It was what Steven needed given that laughter is the best medicine, allegedly.

Unknown to Donna, there was another reason they went for lunch and a pint. He had arranged to meet someone from the online group. It was the lad, Gary, who helped in the car park attacks.

Gary had asked Steven to meet for a pint. Steven, being Mr Nice Guy, chose The Fox in Castle Drum. He knew it was a favourite of Donna's. He was fully aware she didn't get there as often as she liked, even though it was only down the road. Gary had things to discuss. He knew already that Donna would be there and could be trusted. As the pints of cider went down, the stress eased and the excitement of what Gary had shared kicked in.

Chapter 5

He buzzed with excitement. The day he had been looking forward to for so long had finally arrived. He was like a child on Christmas Eve who waited anxiously on Santa Claus. The delivery date he had marked on the kitchen calendar had eventually come around. He was up earlier than usual that morning, just in case the courier arrived at the crack of dawn. Deep down, he knew that would never happen. It was always in the evening, going by previous experience.

Gary was obsessed with computers, and today he was waiting on the godfather of them all. High specifications of everything. Top of the range processor, graphics cards and loaded with RAM—Random Access Memory. This computer would take anything he wanted to throw at it. He had held on long enough to get his hands on it and couldn't wait to install his preferred operating system, Linux. He didn't like or trust Windows and used an open-source operating system that was instruction-based. Linux was the best and most used open-source in the market.

Having cleaned the workstation from all his older equipment the previous night, the space stood empty. He hadn" seen it like that for many years. His old PC had reached the end of its life. It was time for its journey to the cyber graveyard, never to connect to the world again. He had expected this because of the many hardware issues that even he couldn" repair.

Under normal circumstances, he could never have afforded the PC that he sat waiting for. But all that changed six days ago when he picked up just short of six thousand pounds for a six-team football accumulator at the bookmakers. He selected the winning teams and picked both to score in the English premier league and championship. It was a celebration, even though he had spent more than that on losing bets over the last two years.

He was sorry to see the old PC go. He had an emotional attachment to it; they had done so much together. Some people are as sad to see their old cars replaced. Saying goodbye to so many memories can be emotional; this was how Gary felt. It was a day of mixed emotions, even for the toughest of geeks like him. He suffered from the withdrawal symptoms of having no access to a PC and only a phone for company, which was as good as a drum kit to Anne Frank. He couldn't access the places he used to feed his addiction from and that passed most of the day at home over his days off.

He started a deep clean on his London flat. The man was spotless. A simple thing like an unwashed plate in the sink would stress him. He sat busy on his PC, unable to pull himself away, although the plate annoyed him.

His flat was modern. He had a thing for white and chrome. His work station was a chrome tower with a glass desk, two glass shelves underneath and two smaller ones to the left and right, with lighting fitted under each part of the stand. The desk was positioned at the opposite end of the living room from his TV intentionally. That way, it wouldn't distract him while he was working. That's was what he called it. The law called it hacking.

Gary McDonald was a hacktivist. At thirty-two years old, he had moved from Glasgow to London for work. He was a security expert for a website domain company, so going to work was like a busman's holiday; doing something he loved and being paid for it. He enjoyed his job and getting up for work was never a challenge. He was always enthusiastic and full of energy with a great relationship between him and his colleagues. He was also popular with his outgoing character. Always up for a chat, telling jokes, entertaining the crowds, or playing to the audience.

He would work twelve hours a day and be first in and last out of the office. He had the flexibility of four days a week and took home a decent salary, which helped him afford his monthly instalments on his dream car, a black E-class Mercedes. The Mercedes was above his budget, but he liked to dream big. With careful financial management, he secured the car with a bank loan. He also had a mortgage to pay and was living comfortably in the south of Castle Drum, but normally he wouldn't spend almost four thousand on the PC, which was due in the next few hours.

It was his lucky day. At just after eleven that morning, he saw the courier van pull up at the front of his flat. He danced his way to the front door. The only music was in his head. He had the door opened before the delivery driver had even unloaded the package from the van.

Being computer educated in many fields, he had his new PC up and running in no time. Soon all his most used software, including Linux, was downloaded. He made an early lunch while the software was downloading. Finally, it was complete. He sat back in his black leather desk chair, stretched his arms above his head, and let out an enormous sigh.

'Welcome to my world,' he said to his PC.

It must be a geek thing talking to your PC, he thought with a slight smile.

Before his old PC quit, Gary was engrossed in a minor operation, working with a few friends he met online. He had created a database of the UK mainstream media, politicians, and celebrities. All neatly indexed in an excel document he still had on his external hard drive, something that was to him like the Bible is to practising Christians. It was his life. He had gathered information on people over many years, from when he first started his operation, until that current date.

A few weeks previously, he had monitored the negative press about an MP in the House of Commons, Roger Blackwood. This MP was doing nothing except sleeping on the job. Further research revealed that although he was a working MP for the leftist UK Labour Party, he never actually took part in any voting and never asked questions. Gary wanted to get out of there and share the news with Blackwood's constituency. These people voted him in with all the promises under the sun, but in reality, he had done fuck all. This made Gary extremely angry about how

Blackwood could get away with it continuously. He was picking up a considerable salary and expenses for doing absolutely nothing. Gary knew that nobody else would be so lucky in employment. He had witnessed people being sacked and thrown to the wolves for nothing during his career.

Gary was a big lad. Not a muscular bodybuilding type, just a naturally big unit. His sister used to wind him up saying he was a double for the Hollywood actor, The Rock.

There is a common phrase where people say that no one man can change the world. Friends of Gary say that if anyone can change the world, it will be him.

In his circle, everyone agreed about society and how filthy wealthy bankers and giant corporations had destroyed it, which, in a nutshell, was through greed. It took a lot to get Gary angry, but this topic of conversation got his back up. If anyone didn't know him and got into a debate, his knowledge would change their opinion in around ninety percent of discussions. He was a fountain of knowledge.

As well as doing his own research, he was also part of the underground group Anonymous. He decided which two days of the week to take off work, spending the time at home, or maybe one night he would head to a local bar. He was never one to frequent nightclubs and stood strong against the peer pressure of his six mates, unsuccessfully trying to convince him the night was still young after eleven at night. A few beers were enough for him. That's the way he always has been.

In the group Anonymous, he was like their online commander-in-chief. Everyone knew him. He had a fan base from all over the world. He received daily emails of support from as far away as New Zealand. Gary had started the group six years ago with his six drinking buddies. After a few years, the group now peaked at 6,596 members from all parts of the globe. One person added someone else. Only people with the same agenda and who could be trusted would be added. Every friend associated with that person would be removed if anyone broke the rules.

He had amassed details of everyone in the group. Online moniker, nearest major city, age, contact details, who added them and who they added. He even went to the trouble of colour coding each member on a scale of troublemakers. Green was good, yellow was one to watch, orange meant previously caused trouble, and red was the last warning.

He was happy that in the years the group had been running, only one person made it to red, and no one had been removed. They knew what the group was capable of should they turn out to be a snitch. Everyone got on well. They liked the competition in hacking companies, sharing details online, and getting praised. The bigger the company or damage, the more recognition they gained.

Three years ago, Gary had made global headlines when he hacked the Twitter account of the UK pharmaceutical company, Medicod UK, based in London. The company had made the headlines worldwide for putting up the cost of drugs for cancer patients six hundred percent, which had a considerable impact on the NHS.

That evening, after spending the entire day on his PC, he fell asleep on the sofa around eight. Because of this, he was wide awake at four thirty-four the following morning and started the day early. He pulled his favourite energy drink out of the fridge. A morning coffee or tea wasn't strong enough. As usual, he sat behind his twenty-eight-inch monitor.

He had been recently following the story of Medicod UK on the news over the last few days. The company's CEO was Colin Oscar-Douglas, hence the COD at the end of Medi, who was an arrogant prick of a man. He just didn't give a fuck about anyone or what anyone thought of him. He loved the stage, the media spotlight, and saw himself as a bit of a celebrity. A pharmaceutical CEO behaving like a celebrity? Even the Simpsons cartoon couldn't develop that idea, but this was a modern-day society.

Although he loved the spotlight, the public and the media hated the man. Many detested his attitude, but he was really untouchable. Many journalists in the UK took time to dig some dirt on him, but they found nothing. Gary thought it was time to take some action, albeit illegal. Something needed to be done to bring him down a notch or two.

Highly experienced, it wasn't long before Gary connected to the servers that hosted the Medicod UK website. Within a few minutes, he accessed the company data that made up their website. He sat for a few moments in deep thought about what changes he could make to the website. Within a few minutes, he had opened Photoshop and created a picture of Colin Oscar-Douglas being electrocuted. Other images of him were behind bars in prison. An image with a sign that said Tower of London Awaits You, and one where he was the devil in disguise.

This was good enough for that time in the morning. It only took a few minutes before he deleted the entire website's contents. All that remained was the homepage and the four images at the bottom of that page. He also left a note at the bottom of the page that said:

Colin, we have been watching you. We are still watching you.

You have had an abhorrent attitude for a while now and shouldn't be in such a responsible position. You have complete disregard for other people's lives and unjustified inflated drugs prices, which means that you have blood on your hands as now the NHS has to choose who lives and who dies; many more are dying since your ridiculous price increase.

No matter how much money you have, life is a gift that your pounds can't buy. You are not God and will not decide who lives and who dies because of the affordability of the NHS. Our corrupt government might turn a blind eye, as we know many have invested in health care; we, on the other hand, can never allow that.

We have a plan that will disrupt your company and your personal life, and that of your own family. We have an extensive database of each and every one of them. Did you know that your father goes to the shooting gallery every Tuesday evening with his friend Bobby? We do!

This is the first warning. We won't sit back and watch you being cocky and making jokes as if everything in the world is fine. You are killing people. You have forty-eight hours from when this site was taken over to lower the price of life-saving drugs and relieve the pressure on our priceless national health service, or we will initiate phase two and show you that we are not fucking around.

Do the right thing.

We are anonymous. We are Legion. We do not forgive. We do not forget.

Expect us!

Gary sat back, smiling and with a sense of achievement. He felt good about himself and thought about what would be the next step. Gary liked to plan things. So, he provisionally planned phase two and got others involved, should Colin ignore his polite request.

Phase one was now complete and he was feeling hungry. He set a stopwatch on his PC at forty-seven hours and fifty-seven minutes. The time was six zero three. It was now time for breakfast.

Chapter 6

Anonymous became known across the globe. Both left-wing and right-wing activists are using the name these days. Governments were, and still are, terrified of them for a straightforward reason. They didn't know their enemy.

To better understand the group, the majority didn't meet up once a month and have a few beers and talk tech. Maybe a few lived near one and another, but they really were what it says on the tin.

The group consists of anyone interested in activism or hacktivism, as it's known. Wikipedia described them as a decentralised international hacktivist group widely known for its various DDOS cyber-attacks against governments, government institutions, government agencies, corporations and the Church of Scientology, which originated in 2003. Corporate targets have included PayPal, MasterCard, Visa and Sony. They have also publicly supported WikiLeaks. Gary had a role to play in a big way.

As he walked into The Fox bar, Gary noticed Steven and Donna immediately and introduced himself to Donna.

'So, you're the lucky woman who has changed my mate's life?' he said with a cheeky smile and winking at Steven.

Unprepared for such a remark and not knowing who Gary was, she quickly scoffed in a way that was totally out of character.

'And you are?'

Gary laughed, introduced himself, and offered to get a round of drinks in. 'Ciders all round, is it?'

After the bullshit, the getting to know you small talk with Donna and the quick completion of his first pint, all three were getting along great. Lots of laughing and political jokes followed, but they weren't there for just a laugh. Donna went to get the next round of drinks, and that's when Gary started revealing his plan for the next publicity stunt. He wanted to run it past Steven first. Donna also had to be OK with it.

'You've seen them for yourself, mate. I mean, if that was you or I sleeping on the job, earning a fraction of what these MPs take home, we'd be down the job centre the next fucking day. We need to embarrass these lazy bastards.'

He had a hunger to get things rolling quickly.

'Embarrass who?' Donna had caught the tail end of the conversation.

She laid three pints of cider on the table.

'Roger Blackwood. He's the Tory MP for Milford, and he's been taking naps regularly on the job, more than anyone else in fact. We had him monitored. Some of us worked in rotation, attending the public gallery in the House of

Commons. The man has done absolutely nothing. Zero input for anything simply collects his three hundred plus quid a day, and hasn't held a surgery in his constituency for almost six months.'

'So, what are you thinking?'

Over the next round of drinks, Gary explained that if Roger Blackwood liked his sleep that much, they could give him something to sleep on.

The group had been planning over a couple of months, with most taking part via an umbrella group or sub-group, which was set up especially for this project. Around seventeen members had saved up mattresses, bought old ones for pennies, found some at the local dump. One member even placed an ad on Gumtree, requesting old mattresses with free pickup service and insinuated it was for an experimental project in recycling. They had picked up thirty-one from locations up to sixty miles away over the last six weeks. With ninety-six at the last count two days ago, it was almost time.

The plan's first stage was to approach MP Roger Blackwood and have a polite word. To clarify that he is a disgrace, warn him to stop sleeping on the job, tell him to get his finger out of his arse and help his constituents. The members were to inform him he was to be used as an example, which would cause public humiliation, intentionally forgetting to tell him they had in their possession around twenty images from TV screens of him sleeping. Gary thought Donna would be an ideal character for the job.

'So, I just need to catch him coming out of the House of Commons and approach him?'

'No. Four nights a week, he drops into the Anchorage Bar on Summertown Road for one or two before driving home; you can get him there. Go in, tell him the script and leave as soon as possible before he has time to make mental notes about who you are. Wear a baseball cap, put in hair extensions, wear sunglasses, a dust mask, whatever you want. The more protection against your identification, the more it will throw him off track should he decide to report your meeting to the police,' explained Gary.

Steven thought about this for a few minutes. He knew nothing about Donna getting involved until Gary asked her. It all happened quickly. Did he really want Donna involved?

Could he live with the guilt if anything went wrong?

'I'll do it; leave her out of this.' He looked Gary directly in the eyes.

'Not a chance, mate!' Donna put her hand on Steven's arm. 'This is mine, and I'm so up for it; I need to be a part of this. You had your excitement in the car park, Steven. This is nothing dangerous. I will be in and out in minutes. Let's have a drink to my first mission.'

All three were in touch a lot over the next few days. Donna stayed at Steven's most of the time and only returned home for more clothes. She was gradually moving everything into her new home but had plenty of time because of the notice required on her rental agreement. She was waiting anxiously but excitedly for Gary's call, the way Steven felt before his organised attack. Every day since she accepted her role, she walked around Steven's flat reciting what she must say.

It was time. Steven received the call and told Donna to be at the Anchorage Bar at quarter to six that evening.

'I'll come with you for support.' She agreed.

Steven just wanted to make sure she was safe; after all, she was now his woman, and he had fallen in love with her after all these years.

They arrived, but Steven didn't go in. He sat on a bench in the park opposite the bar.

Donna had dressed in jeans, trainers, a black bomber-style jacket and a baseball cap. She wore a dark, long-haired wig underneath. She walked to the door of the Anchorage Bar and took a deep breath. The photo in her hand was the only visual she had. It was a recent picture from online. No one paid attention when she entered; they were glued to their smartphones.

The bar was beautiful. A vast mirrored gantry with what looked like every spirit on the market available. Various whiskies, vodkas and gins were the first things that caught her eye. On a barstool was MP Blackwood. Again, Donna took a deep breath and reassured herself that this was easy and she would be out in minutes.

As she got within twenty feet of him, he turned around and made eye contact. There was now no turning back. The point of no return had arrived, and it was her time to shine.

'Mr Roger Blackwood MP. You are one lazy, useless bastard, and I'm here to give you a warning. The British people are sick and tired of you and many other MPs, and today we are fighting back.'

'Who are you?' He leaned forward, screwing up his eyes.

'I'll explain that in a minute, but listen carefully. We've monitored you over the last few months and discovered that you have slept on the job almost every day over the previous two months. We class this as a dereliction of duties. Now, heed this warning. Should your afternoon naps continue, we will embarrass you on a national level. We are keeping our powder dry for now, but the choice is yours.'

'Is this some kind of joke? Who are you?' Blackwood repeated.

Donna somehow blurted out words that were not in the pre-planned script.

'We are anonymous. We are legion. We do not forgive. We do not forget. Expect us.'

She walked to the exit, fighting the urge to look back and see if she was being followed.

'I'm calling the police; this is threatening behaviour. Who do you think you are? Do you know who I am?' Blackwood raised his voice, making sure everyone could hear.

She pulled the bar door open and darted as fast as she could towards the park to meet Steven. She took a seat on the bench beside him after her hundred-yard sprint. She couldn't stop laughing and struggled to speak. Eventually, in between deep breaths and laughs, she found her voice.

'That was an adrenalin rush if ever there was one!'

Steven looked relieved. Although he didn't want her involved, he wouldn't stand in her way, as that would be nothing short of hypocritical. He didn't want to come across as overprotective. He gave her a hug and congratulated her while thinking how amazing she was. Before they headed back to Steven's flat to share the news with the forum, Donna came up with an idea.

'Go into the pub for a drink yourself, get his reaction, and find out if he really called the police.'

Steven thought for a few seconds, then agreed. Donna waited in the park, and having removed the cap and the wig, going from black hair back to blonde, she felt comfortable enough to stay near the Anchorage. With no police car outside, Steven tried to act normal as he cautiously approached the bar.

'Fucking troublemaking bastards. Is this what the world is coming to? I can't have forty winks at work when what's going on doesn't concern me. It's been going on for decades; it's the norm. These jumped-up youngsters with their technology. They don't know how fucking lucky they have life today, and we gave them the luxury they live in.' Blackwood was ranting to the barman.

'Just a pint of cider, thanks.' Steven's voice didn't waver.

Minding his own business, he stared into the gantry of the bar in awe at the size of it. Facing a full one hundred and eighty degrees from Blackwood, he heard his shouts,

'Fucking animals! Do you know what happened just minutes before you arrived? Excuse me, you, yes, you.' Steven turned round to look him right in the eyes.

'Sorry, can you say that again? I was daydreaming.'

'Them fucking Anonymous just threatened me.' His voice told Steven he'd had more than the usual one or two drinks this evening.

'What are you talking about? I don't understand; what's Anonymous?' Steven's confused look gave nothing away.

He listened to Blackwood for almost fifteen minutes. Steven remembered that Donna was in the park as the MP raged about online terrorists. He made his excuse to leave.

'I'm sorry, but I need to leave; this was just a quick one before my train. My advice would be to call the police if you haven't already.'

'A total waste of police resources; they can't do anything.'

That was his cue to leave. Job done.

'It's been nice to meet you. I hope you have a better evening. Goodbye.'

Steven had been overthinking. He remembered Gary telling him he only had one or two before going home, but couldn't remember if he meant driving home. In the distance, he saw Donna on the park bench and called her.

'Are you OK? Everything is good at this end. He never called the police. Can you stay there for another few minutes? I think he could leave soon. I will explain why when I get there. Just give me five to ten minutes.'

Steven went to the pub's window and stood looking in at Roger Blackwood. He watched him finish his glass of whisky; a double, of course.

Steven filmed him taking the last two sips before saying goodbye to the barman. He left the bar, then walked almost two hundred and fifty yards before he clicked the fob for his car.

Steven was a maximum of fifty yards from him and again recorded him getting in his car. This was a bonus. They never expected this to happen, but the situation just fell into their hands with some quick thinking. This was more ammunition against him. This could go viral, but not just yet.

As he arrived back in the park and reunited with a now freezing Donna, he told her the details. They were both bursting with excitement. They couldn't wait to get home and tell the group what had happened.

Online, Donna was a celebrity. Everyone sent her congratulations, which made her feel part of something. She really enjoyed the attention. After they closed the MacBook for the evening, Steven suggested they call it a night and go to bed.

'Are you tired?'

'I said nothing about going to sleep.'

He massaged her shoulders, rubbed his hand upwards around her neck, and then held her cheek in the palm of his hand before kissing her.

Two days passed before Gary called Steven.

'You won't believe this, but Blackwood was sleeping on the job again yesterday and today. We're going to bring the plan forward and we'll need some muscle. Are you in?'

'In what context do you mean *muscle*?'

'Don't worry, nobody is going to get hurt. Roger lives at fifty-seven Antrim Street in a bungalow. Every Saturday morning, he and his wife go to the local tennis club. When they leave, we arrive and give him something to sleep on. We stopped the collection at one hundred.'

'This is funny as fuck, mate. Count me in, Donna too.' Donna acknowledged by nodding her head, without even knowing what was involved. She trusted Steven's judgement.

'I'll send you a meeting point. Get there at nine-fifteen, and we'll take it from there. We have spotters at his house who will give us the green light when they are out. Speak soon, mate.'

'Do you want to have some fun with mattresses?' joked Steven.

Saturday morning arrived. They were excited. Armed with cameras and gloves for the lifting, they made their way to the meeting point.

'How long does it take to move one hundred urine and cum stained mattresses?'

'There will be a lot of people, so it shouldn't take that long.'

Just at that, a dark blue van pulled up alongside a large white truck.

Gary was in the passenger seat of the truck. He jumped out and opened the back of the blue van. It was full of people, at least thirty, all smiling with excitement.

'We can't have a convoy of vehicles entering a quiet street; the neighbours would be out in seconds. Materials are in the white truck, labour in the blue van. We should do it in minutes.'

The truck driver received the call they had been waiting for. He contacted the van driver, who was parked two minutes away from Antrim Street. Blackwood and his wife had just left. It was time to get the much-discussed plan into action.

'Right, people, you all know the drill. We pull up with the blue van first; the white truck drives by and will partially reverse into the driveway; please stay out of his way for our own safety. Each of you will grab the nearest mattresses from inside with the person next to you and place them longways across the living room window, continuing to the front door and then towards the garage. Then stack. Repeat this process until there are no more mattresses remaining in the white truck. Let's do this!' instructed Gary, with excitement in his voice, a smile on his face.

He was confident it would go like the military operation he had planned.

Steven and Donna jumped into the back of the blue van and squeezed towards the front. It wasn't a long journey. Five minutes maximum. Everyone had a good chat; adrenalin was pumping through their veins. It excited them when they thought how funny this stunt was. They looked forward to the media's reaction and hoped to gain more public support for their actions.

The blue van came to a stop; the driver raised the back shutter, and the group walked the forty feet to the driveway, at a safe distance from the incoming delivery. The white truck reversed up to the driveway's edge with the back wheels on the pavement. Within seconds, the driver was out and opening the rear doors. The smell was the first thing that hit them. It was disgusting. Donna was glad they both had gloves on.

'Right, let's get going, people,' Gary shouted, military-style.

Within thirteen minutes, they had unloaded one hundred mattresses from the large white truck. One unloaded almost every eleven seconds. There was a row of ten long ways, ten high across the front of the house, all the way to the garage. It looked amazing. Some people that Steven didn't know pulled out a box of pictures on A4 paper.

'Scatter these all over the garden and street, quickly.'

These were pictures of Blackwood sleeping in the House of Commons on different occasions. This is what Donna had warned him about in the Anchorage Bar. There must have been at least a ream of A4 paper, enough to give Greenpeace a breakdown. They scattered the images over the garden, the neighbours' gardens and the street. A few examples of the messages included:

We'll give you something to sleep on. Resign now. No sleeping on the job. A waste of salary and a cost to the public purse.

The most important thing was to ensure there were no threats to him or his family. This was something they were confident wouldn't happen in this well-organised umbrella group.

'Everyone back in their transport immediately. We need to take photos.' The shout came from a male on the pavement opposite.

As everyone left, they took photos of their own. It was a fantastic sight. They left Antrim Street with a feeling of accomplishment. Delighted with themselves at how smoothly it went, they needed to get this sent to the UK mainstream media, knowing that they were taking a gamble in hoping the press would find this stunt newsworthy. If other nations picked up on it via the internet, the UK media had no choice. This was what was beautiful about the internet.

Back in the blue van, Donna felt alive. She had done nothing like this in her life before and was loving it. Without as much as a parking ticket, she was new to breaking the law, as was Steven. But he seemed more nervous than her. He was up for the jobs and was more than capable, but still he got a little paranoid.

'What's next? I could do things like this all day and night; it's such a fucking buzz, although I just wish I could be a fly on the wall to see their reaction when they get back; how good would that be? Eh, Steven?'

He thought to himself that it was his fault she was now involved, and it was going to take a lot of persuading for her to take a back seat.

'Well, that's the thing, Donna. You will get to see their reaction.' He gave her a cheeky smile and a wink.

'About now, one of the team, I can't remember his name, is to park his car on the other side of the road from their house, take the wheel off and make-believe he's changing a tyre, the car has two cameras on board.'

Donna's mouth just fell open; she was speechless for a few seconds.

'Do you guys think of fucking everything? This is outstanding. I hope the car is close enough to get the audio, too.' She laughed and pretended to slap Steven on both cheeks.

Back at Steven's flat, they collapsed onto the couch. They avoided the news channels showing the global premiere of their latest stunt. They just wanted to relax, watch a movie, and forget about everything else for the rest of the day. Steven was also thinking about how much he enjoyed himself with Donna in his life more often. Also, he was halfway through his holiday from work. He thought about whether to go back.

Just as the movie finished, they simultaneously received a video by DM. It was Roger Blackwood and his wife returning home from tennis.

'I will find these bastards if it's with my last breath, horrible bastards.'

He dragged the mattresses away one by one until he had made a pathway to his house.

'You're telling me you saw and heard nothing? I don't believe you!' Roger shouted at the next-door neighbour. This was gold. They watched it several times and gave each other a high five before starting another movie.

After an hour's nap, they woke up and watched around twenty minutes of the second movie. Coffee was required or they would both go back to sleep and waste the rest of the day.

'Be a good lad and put the kettle on, Steven. I'll have a quick shower.'

He did as he was asked, then sauntered through to the living room where he waited on some news; there was next to nothing. Only a few hundred posts on Twitter, which all had the leading UK newspapers tagged, but nothing appeared on the media's own accounts or newspapers. It looked as though their stunt was being ignored. Not newsworthy by the top brass editors at the mainstream media, the ones who were in the pockets of the government.

Steven thought about it and called Gary.

'Nothing big on Twitter, lad; it's like it never happened; where do we go from here?' asked a diffused Steven.

'Can you send me the two videos of him drinking and then driving?' Gary asked. 'We'll get that out and, if there are enough of the group online, there is a slight chance we can get it to start trending in around an hour. I'm so happy that you used your initiative and got that footage; this is what could ignite the full story. Without that, it could have been a total waste of time.'

As Gary requested, Steven posted the videos to the group. It was gold, right enough. An investigation by the police would be the minimum requirement they expected. The videos were posted on Twitter within minutes with the local police constabulary tags from Anonymous Twitter accounts.

This time, it was obvious; Blackwood had committed a crime. Replies to the main drink driving post were pictures of the house blocked with piss-stained mattresses and flyers lying all over the street. In the forum, the main post discussed Blackwood's drink driving antics, there were pictures of the afternoon's events at his home. His crime couldn't be ignored, mainly because the media followed the main Anonymous account, which was only active for specialist subjects' projects, and was not used daily. One hour and seven minutes passed, and there it was for the world to see.

Milford MP faces drink driving allegations by online group, Anonymous was the headline on Twitter, Facebook and the Daily Mail's website. Every media outlet had followed suit and covered the story. It was all over the UK media within an hour, and it was all down to Steven's quick thinking. It wasn't long before the coverage extended to the MP's home and a garden full of mattresses.

The public backlash about sleeping on the job was massive, with the majority commenting on how they would be sacked if they slept on the job. It was even discussed on many morning chats shows the following day that MPs should lose their three hundred pounds per day if we caught them sleeping at work. Discussions about MPs being made more accountable were high on the media agenda. Steven thought that while he became nervous during these stunts, it really made a difference, and things were being brought to light. While the media were doing their job for a change, they were next in the firing line.

Chapter 7

He slipped out of bed and went into the shower without waking Donna. Standing with his head bent under the steaming hot water in his glass and chrome shower area with black tiled walls, he thought about going back to work. He had almost arrived at the end of his holiday period; only two more days remained. He didn't want to go back. As much as the anxiety and paranoia had got to him recently, spending all day and night with Donna and being involved with the group was the most exciting times he had in years. Some people went abroad for a good time, and there was Steven, who had had the time of his life in the surrounding areas of his home town. He could always make enquiries and see how the office was coping. Did they really need him?

Twenty minutes under the shower passed quickly, mostly in deep thought, rather than washing. Steven went to the kitchen naked and put the kettle on.

'Maybe I should just call them, and then I will know one way or another,' he said out loud. His inner voice replied as he debated with himself.

He picked up his phone and messaged Jason, his good friend at work.

You lot managing without me? He sent it via WhatsApp.

Almost immediately, he got a reply.

Worse than usual, not much happening; how's your time off?

He never replied to that message. This was his moment to call the office and speak to the boss, his father's friend.

'Hey Matt. How are you?'

After a little small talk, Steven dropped the question.

'So, do you think you'd miss me for another couple of weeks if I was to take some unpaid leave?' he asked.

A silence seemed to go on longer than the four seconds it actually took.

'Steven, if I'm honest with you, you would be doing the company a favour; you know I wouldn't sack you, but times are tough, so take as long as you want,' Matt replied.

After wishing him all the best, Steven put the phone down, let out a sigh of relief, and smiled. He had the answer he was looking for. Steven could afford unpaid leave. Although he wasn't loaded with cash, he had enough in the bank for a comfortable life. His father had bought him the flat, so he had no rent to pay. He jumped back into bed, now fully clothed, and grabbed hold of Donna. She woke up immediately.

'Good morning, gorgeous!' He started with a calm voice, then shouted, 'Come on, get up; what time is this to sleep?

You're missing a beautiful morning. I've got a surprise for you.'

He pulled the duvet from Donna and pretended to push her out of bed.

'Go away, please. Leave me alone. I need more sleep,' Donna pleaded, while placing one hand over his cheek and giving it a slight rub.

'Have you ever been to Amsterdam?' Steven knew full well she had never been out of the country.

'No, you know I haven't.'

Donna was now more awake and paying attention.

'What if I told you I'm going to book a few days in Amsterdam for us right after you get out of bed?' Steven had a massive grin on his face.

Donna threw the duvet over Steven's head and jumped out of bed.

'I'm up, I'm up!' she shouted.

'OK, I'll book it and you make breakfast. Deal?' Steven suggested, even though making breakfast was the straightforward part of the deal. Toast, coffee and freshly squeezed orange juice weren't that difficult.

'Tell me you are serious?' Donna stood in her white nightdress and placed her hands placed on her heart, waiting for a reply.

'I'm one hundred percent serious. Let's spend some real quality time together.'

They hadn't much planned for the afternoon. Maybe shopping and then take the dog to either his brother's or his dad's. Surely one of them wouldn't mind looking after Ben while they were in Amsterdam. It was time for everyone to know that he was now in a serious relationship with Donna, and whichever one knew first, they would tell the other. If his dad wasn't going off on holiday, he would be the preferred option. With a massive garden, it would have been less hassle than making sure his brother took the dog for a walk.

'Dad, how are you?' Steven spoke first.

After the usual chitchat, he discovered his dad would be staying at home, and he agreed to look after Ben. They agreed to drop him off in an hour.

'Flights are expensive because it's short notice,' joked Steven.

'Why don't we just go next week? When are you going back to work?' Donna asked.

'I'm off work for the foreseeable future.'

Steven explained the call he made to Matt while she was still asleep.

'OK, change of plan. We're leaving tonight. It's only forty pounds of a difference between flight prices, and there's no time like the present. Get packing, gorgeous. We're off to Amsterdam.'

Steven got up from the couch and hugged Donna.

That afternoon, he visited his mother and father, who were delighted to see that they were a happy couple. His mother remarked that she always hoped they would get together. She loved Donna and her family. They spent a few hours chatting, and his parents wished them all the best and told them to enjoy their holiday. His dad slipped him fifty pounds to have a meal and a drink on them. It was time they headed to the airport.

Donna was nervous. She hadn't flown before, so Steven suggested a few drinks in the airport departures bar. They had five minutes short of an hour to get to the London Gatwick to Amsterdam gate, time for a couple of ciders. She loved the flight and realised she had been nervous for no reason. They were hyper with excitement. Amsterdam was also a first for Steven. He had been to many other countries but never The Netherlands.

As they arrived at Schiphol Airport, the size of the place amazed them. It was massive. Like a shopping centre with a train station underneath the central airport plaza. After buying train tickets, they made their way underground. Trains to Amsterdam Central were every ten minutes, with a ten to fifteen-minute walk along the main street called the Damrak to the hotel Steven had booked. In her excitement, Donna had forgotten to ask about the hotel.

On Damrak, Donna looked to the left.

'Wow! Check that hotel out! It looks posh!' It was an old building, spectacularly lit up with giant national flags hanging from the top. The massive gleaming glass entrance had revolving doors. 'That's out of this world,' she continued.

'Let's have a closer look; it's on the way to our hotel,' Steven pulled her hand.

It was dark, but Donna insisted on taking pictures. Dam Square was behind her, with Madame Tussauds on the other side of the road from the square. She finished up with pictures of the entrance and the flags on the roof of the Amsterdam Grand Hotel Krasnapolsky.

'Shall we check in now, gorgeous?' Steven asked, pointing to the shimmering revolving doors.

Donna stood still, looking between Steven and building in front of her.

'Yeah, right, you *are* joking!' She shook her head. As well as never having been out of the country, Donna hadn't stayed in many hotels. This was all new to her.

'This is our hotel. I'm serious. Let's go.' Steven pulled his luggage with one hand and grabbed Donna's hand with the other.

Inside, the Dutch receptionist welcomed them and told them they had a free upgrade to the King Suite on the top floor. As they entered what they thought was a room, Donna's mouth fell open. It was a small apartment with a separate living area from the main ensuite bedroom. It was beautiful; bright with modern furniture. The stunning views from the sixth floor captured their interest immediately.

It had been a long day. After a few drinks in the hotel bar, they had an early night once planning on waking up fresh to see Amsterdam after breakfast. Steven switched on the TV and searched for a music channel until he found a chilled eighties station with romantic music. He stripped off and jumped into bed as Donna came out of the bathroom.

'Love you,' said Steven, waiting on Donna's reaction.

'I love you too, Mr Walker.' She jumped into bed with a huge smile.

It was a big moment for Steven, and he felt a tremendous sense of relief. He had wanted to tell her he loved her for so long, but was always afraid of the reaction. Although things were different with Donna now, he still felt insecure, a legacy from his previous relationships. Steven placed his left arm under Donna's neck and his right arm around her waist, giving her a tight hug.

'I just love your cuddles,' she reassured him.

The sound of breathing interrupted the silence. She turned to face him, and they both began kissing with speed and passion. Within minutes, they threw the bedsheets to the floor and made mad, passionate love for the next hour.

They woke early and, after more sex in the shower, it was time for breakfast and to explore Amsterdam. The first stop was Madame Tussauds, which excited Donna. But they were more excited about their pre-booked visit to the Heineken factory, where they could hear the story of Heineken. Although they both preferred cider, Heineken was one beer they enjoyed occasionally.

Later that afternoon, they sat in the bar at The Heineken Experience. The tour had been amazing. A guide gave them the story of Mr Heineken's start and how he overcame his struggle to create one of the world's best-known beers. They learned something that day. After cashing in their tokens, they drank a few small glasses of fresh beer in the bar. It had been made on the same premises less than twenty-four hours before. They agreed the refreshing liquid was worth every penny, then left through the gift shop, resisting the temptation to buy more beer.

'Do you know anyone from the group over here?' asked a curious Donna.

'No, I don't think so; I have spoken to people from Holland, but I'm not sure of their exact location.'

'Maybe we should ask if anyone is here, and we can meet up? I mean, when are we going to be back here? We could find out what the group here is working on and get some ideas,' Donna suggested.

'That's a good plan, but I thought we wanted to get away from everything for a couple of days and just switch off?' Her request surprised Steven.

'It's just a thought. Maybe we can enjoy a couple of days and then meet someone on the last day?'

'I could always give Gary a call; he knows people here without a doubt.'

Having spent most of their time walking a distance from the hotel, they saw most of what they had come for. Coffee shops were difficult to find these days. The red-light district had become a fraction of the size it was fifteen years before, but they still had a great time before Steven brought out his phone.

'Gary, how are you doing?' Steven asked.

After chatting for so long, his coffee was cold. Donna had drunk hers and waited patiently.

'We can meet someone from the group today,' Steven told her.

Gary sent Steven's number to a Dutch mate, Karl Smit, who would be in contact that afternoon.

'Is Karl based in Amsterdam?' Donna asked.

'No, he's from Haarlem. It's only a short train journey for him; we can meet him in our hotel bar.'

After a day on their feet, covering more than a few kilometres, hunger drove them to something sweet and fattening. The pancakes in the shop on Damrak were massive. Their order arrived, covered in chocolate and banana. They shared one and asked for more coffee, determined to finish it.

Steven's phone rang.

'Hello, is that Steven?' a voice asked.

'Yes, I see it's a Dutch number. Are you Karl?'

They agreed to meet at the hotel in forty minutes. Karl was already on the train.

'What shall we ask him? It was my idea to meet someone, and now I'm getting nervous,' said Donna.

'Don't be silly, just be ourselves, and we can share stories, learn how to deal with things. According to Gary, Karl is one of the most respected hacktivists in the Netherlands.' Donna shivered at the thought of some online VIP in the presence of their company.

One crucial thing stood out for both Steven and Donna. It was a challenge to find cider in the bars. Beer was everywhere. Of course there was cider, but never on draught, and cans of cider tasted different. Back at the hotel, the bar beckoned them. They ordered two pints of Heineken and took seats next to the window, looking out over the massive square. Normally, it was full of tourists who visit each year. Holland coped with seventeen million each year from all over the world.

'I bet that's Karl over there.' Donna had noticed a small but medium-built man with short black hair and wearing glasses walking towards the hotel entrance. A geeky-looking man on his own.

'We'll soon find out,' Steven said as the man got closer to the revolving doors.

He walked into the hotel, straight past reception, and entered the bar. After looking around, he saw one man sitting alone. Steven and Donna were obviously who he wanted. He walked towards them, smiling.

'Steven and Donna?' he quizzed.

'You must be Karl.' Steven stood up, extended his hand and gave Karl a firm handshake.

'And you must be the amazing Donna that I've read about!'

Donna stood up to shake his hand, but Karl moved forward to kiss her cheek. Not once, not twice, but three times. This confused Donna, so she pulled away after the second kiss.

'It's a Dutch thing, three kisses on the cheek,' explained Karl as he continued to tell them the different number of kisses given in other countries. 'We're not weird, just different; we are a friendly bunch here in Holland.' He laughed.

Steven suggested a round of drinks and Karl settled for a Heineken.

'I'll go to the bar.' Donna left them to continue their introduction of small talk.

Four pints later, they were having a great time at the plush hotel bar. On first impressions, Karl was a good guy. He knew what he was talking about; he knew his stuff, both online and in reality. The Dutchman told them stories from the last few years and how the group had come from nothing. He was not a founding member, but joined when members were fifty strong. He had an excellent relationship with Gary and had previously met up a few times in England.

Karl continued telling stories about previous stunts the group had carried out over the years and the actual changes in people's lives. They began targeting many CEOs of companies employing people on the minimum wage and had terrible working conditions. One CEO eventually got pissed off, continually looking over his shoulder, so he gave the employees a pay rise. The group soon realised they had power in numbers and used technology to their advantage to carry out the publicity stunts.

Karl explained that hacking company databases and internal servers had been their golden ticket back in the day, but although security was getting tighter, there was always a way in. It was a game of cat and mouse with cyber security firms. They could spend weeks hacking company servers, but they could do whatever they wanted when they eventually gained access. The time:reward ratio was worth it.

All this impressed Steven. Although he knew what he was doing online daily, Karl was a champion's league hacktivist. He took in the information Karl was sharing. Stunt ideas, computer knowledge, contacts, meeting places. Donna just listened as she sat on her phone. Steven had suggested things to Karl that he thought would be too outrageous, like taking down security systems to enter buildings. Karl informed Steven that a group had previously accomplished this task during the break-in of an Austrian pharmaceutical company building many years ago. This was music to Steven's ears. He had so many plans, and the biggest hurdle was gaining access to the buildings.

Karl headed back to his hometown of Haarlem, and Steven and Donna went up to the hotel room. Although Donna had sat on her phone and let Steven do the talking, she had paid attention.

'So, do you think we can use some of his ideas back in the UK?' Donna asked Steven.

'Of course. He has some great ideas; let's hope I remember them tomorrow after we have this last joint.' Steven laughed.

'You see, Steven, this is why women are more organised than men.'

'Meaning?'

'Well, you don't really think I sat on social medial being anti-social while you were both chatting now, did you? I made notes. All the important points of the conversation are in my little notebook!'

'You never fail to amaze me, honey; I would never have thought about that. Let's get back to the UK and start putting together our next plan of action. The one with smoke at the end sounds amusing.' They giggled.

Chapter 8

A t the flat, Donna looked at her Amsterdam pictures on Steven's laptop. She loved the trip and thought about how much time she had wasted, not travelling anywhere further than Scotland. Even then, that was only on one occasion many years ago to visit an old friend. It wasn't the fact Donna feared flying or going other places; it simply just didn't cross her mind. She was happy and content in her life, but now she was older and had her first experience abroad, she wanted more. She realised that more holidays would only be possible if she could find a better job.

'What was your best moment in Amsterdam?' Donna asked Steven, who was watching TV.

'If I'm sincere, it could have been any city in the world; just spending time with you was the most important thing for me,' he said, without taking his eyes off the TV.

'Awe, you're just so sweet. That's such a nice thing to say.'

She got up from the table, walked towards Steven, leaned over the back of the couch, and gave him a hug and a quick kiss.

'What are we doing today?' she whispered.

'How about lunch and a few pints? Let's see if any of the group are around. We can share the information from Karl with them.'

'The Fox Bar?' she begged him. She loved their lasagne and chips.

'Yes, we can do that. I'll give Gary a call and see if he's free.'

He grabbed hold of her and pulled her over the couch and onto his knee. They lay down on the couch and hugged.

'Five-minute cuddle, then we will make a move?'

Donna acknowledged him with a smile as they got comfortable on the couch.

With his feet on the desk chatting shit about football to his workmate, Gary was passing the time at work. Not much was going on in the office, but he clocked the hours up. He couldn't be bothered. The previous night had been a long one rather than a late one. He was in bed by twelve-fifteen and had spent the time hacking a tourist company database. He added household names in mass numbers. One thousand Charles Chaplin's with no additional information. Two thousand Mr B Beans, a few thousand Michael Mouses. He spent a while adding many celebrity names to their database, at least two hundred thousand files in one dump. That would cause massive disruption to any company. To Gary, it was an act of revenge.

This small-time travel agent had ripped a few family members off and, after various attempts at getting a refund, the owner told them they were getting fuck all refund. Not the best customer service when people are down a few thousand pounds.

Gary had also emailed twelve travel company accounts. He sent basic instructions. Pay refunds or further attacks would occur on their systems. He informed them that their security was weak, and he had placed an entry point that he could access. Even by upgrading their protection, they still wouldn't find his entry point. They could take the gamble, but if they did not issue the refunds in forty-eight hours from the time stamp on the email, he would destroy their entire server, and all the information they held would be passed on to local rival tourist companies.

As he packed his rucksack, Gary's phone rang with the sound of his favourite movie soundtrack, the ringtone from Wolf Alice and the chorus of their track Silk. He loved it. It differed from anything else he listened to. He let it ring until he finished packing the last of his things and picked it up with SW flashing on the screen.

'Steven, how are you doing, mate?' Gary asked.

'I'm alright, mate, so much to discuss after meeting Karl in The Dam. Are you up for lunch and a few cold ones?'

'I'm leaving the office as I speak; twelve minutes and I'll be there.'

'Twelve minutes? Not ten, not fifteen, twelve?'

It was fifteen minutes by bus. That was if the bus arrived as soon as they got to the bus stop. Steven called a taxi, which would be there in minutes. He and Donna arrived eleven minutes after the phone call. Gary arrived thirteen minutes after the phone call, just as he said he would.

'You're a minute late!' Steven laughed.

'I never considered the traffic lights on Mill Road.' Gary kissed Donna on the cheek and said hello to them both.

After ordering food and drinks, they took the same seats as on their last visit, next to the window, but still with a good view of the televisions around the bar.

'How did you get on with Karl?' asked Gary.

'He's a great guy.' Steven and Donna answered simultaneously.

'He really knows his stuff,' said Steven.

'He gave us some great ideas. Can we get on the next case soon? I got a buzz from him, and it feels like months since we did anything, although it's not even been two weeks,' Donna said.

'We have a few things lined up, but nothing big is ready to go. We have a bit of destruction planned if you two are up for it.'

'What kind of destruction? More car parks? Buildings? Graffiti?' Steven sounded excited.

'We have discussed it as destruction, but I prefer to call it a money-saving exercise,' Gary turned serious. 'It's the NHS. Don't you think it's a disgrace that doctors, nurses and families should have to pay parking fees visiting sick patients?'

'It's a nightmare trying to park; my mum had to park nearly a mile away on her last appointment and almost arrived late. She was in a right panic.' Donna explained.

'The group has been discussing it for over a year now. Some say it will cut down on free-for-all parking, others say the costs are too high and more say it serves the purpose. So, it really has split the group,' said Gary.

'When is this happening, and what are the plans?' asked Steven.

'Well, it's pretty simple; we just destroy the pay points. Some are outside the hospital, and some are inside at the reception. We pour Nitromors inside them. It will corrode the insides, rendering them useless. It'll take weeks or even months for them to be replaced, depending on the level of red tape they need to go through ordering replacements.' explained Gary. 'We target the busiest hospitals; we can't do as many as we'd like across the UK as some are already free in Scotland, and on this task, we don't really have the support in the group as I already mentioned.'

'I'm in,' said Donna.

Steven nodded approval.

'To change the subject for a minute, do you know the story about the smoke bombs and the Dutch media Karl and the team carried out?' Steven looked at Gary.

'That was outrageous and took a lot of work, but the result was superb.'

'Can we do it in the UK? I think it would be amazing,' Donna asked.

'There's a few of the troops interested in doing it, it's just that nobody has taken the lead in getting the wheels in motion. In the group, the problem is everyone has these amazing ideas, but only a small majority will actually get off their arses, research, and put in the hard groundwork.

Many just want things put on a plate, and they join in and follow instructions.' explained Gary.

'We could do this, Steven, our own project right from the start; what do you think?' Donna waited for an answer.

Steven said nothing. After a long pause, he pulled a face that showed the other two he was thinking about it. The conversation continued between Donna and Gary.

It was then Steven heard the excitement in Donna's voice. She was telling Gary about new ideas.

What if? What if something went wrong? He had waited years to get into the relationship he had with Donna. Could he risk it? What if he lost her to a holiday courtesy of Her Majesty's Prison services? Or even *he* could end up in prison. If he didn't go along with something that he got her involved with in the first place, would she still hang around? They were together now and enjoyed the same interests, from music to movies, from food to activism.

'Let's do it then.' Steven interrupted them both mid-sentence.

'The smoke stunts?' asked Donna.

'Yes, let's do it. Fuck it.' This delighted Donna and Gary.

'Cause for celebration. Another cider?'

Gary went towards the bar.

'We need as much information as we can from Karl and his group. They have already done this, and they will have good advice. Maybe he would share some information about things they would do differently a second time,' said Donna.

'I'll call him, and we can chat about it online. Maybe he still has some useful documents on file.'

Gary arrived back holding three pints of cider. He placed them on the table while listening to his ringtone from his pocket. He pulled out the phone.

'It's my sister; I need to take this.' He walked a few feet away from the table. 'Hi, sis, how are you?'

There was a pause as he listened.

'Yes, that's great news. I'm please for you. Are you going to book somewhere else?' Gary enquired. 'OK, that will save me going down to the shop and smashing his face in.'

Gary laughed as the call ended.

'My sister, she got ripped off from a travel agent who refused to refund her, but it's sorted now; she's getting her money back in the next few days. I love a happy ending,' He smiled.

'And would Mr Gary have anything to do with that?' asked Donna.

Gary described himself in the third person. 'He might have accessed their database last night and made a few changes! I hacked their system and borrowed a copy of their full database and then replaced it with some modifications.'

He then explained exactly what he had done and the conditions they were to follow. If they paid all the money back to the families, then he would return everything on the database to normal within the next twenty-four hours. They wouldn't hear from him ever again. Gary wouldn't know when everyone was paid, but he would restore things when his family members were refunded. It was all about his sister and her family this time.

At that point, Steven had a minor explosion go off inside his head, like a bit of firework display of thoughts. His reaction grabbed the attention of both Donna and Gary.

'What's wrong, honey?' asked Donna.

'When did you hack the travel agents?' Steven watched Gary.

'I worked on it most of last night and then went to bed.'

'What time did you go to bed?' Steven asked with curiosity.

'Er, er, I can't remember, quarter past twelve maybe.'

Steven looked directly into Gary's eyes, put his hands over his face, and laughed.

'No, it couldn't be. I just had this thought. It's something that's been on my mind for a while now. There are too many coincidences and comments from people that I'm adding up. I could be wrong, but...' Steven stopped speaking.

'You've lost me.' Gary shook his head.

'And me,' said Donna.

'OK, I will just come out with it. Are you Midnight Justice?' Steven asked Gary.

Donna sat in shock for a few seconds, with her right hand across her mouth and eyes wide open, before saying, 'Midnight Justice, as in the world-famous Midnight Justice?'

'That exact one, Donna,' said Steven while still staring at Gary.

'That's a huge endorsement and responsibility to have,' Gary replied with a slight grin.

'It's fucking you! Tell the truth!' Steven's voice rose and carried across the quiet pub.

'Would it make any difference if I was?' asked Gary.

'Not really, but if you are him, then why the fuck would you keep that from me?'

'I mean, I have heard of the things Midnight Justice has carried out, but for some reason, I thought he was American because a lot of the action took place in the US,' said Donna.

'You do know that from now on, you are entering an elite club of people.' Gary gave a short, quiet laugh.

'I fucking knew it, my sixth sense told me, and then there were certain things people said that would mean they assumed I already knew your identity.'

'OK, OK, let's calm down.' Gary noticed Steven was almost on the edge of his seat.

'It's me. I'm Midnight Justice.' Gary finally came out with the words.

'Fucking hell,' said Donna.

'I have been drinking with one of the world's greatest hacktivists; I need a more potent drink than this. Who's for Jaeger bombs?' Steven was still in shock as he got up.

'I'll be having a word with you when I get back,' said Steven as he placed his hand on Gary's shoulder and walked towards the bar, shaking his head in disbelief.

Donna sat with Gary in silence. Her head was working overtime. Steven was right. Gary was a great hacktivist.

'So, you can hack just about anything?' asked Donna, trying to bring the uncomfortable silence to an end.

'Just about. I never have, shall we say, been defeated? But I will say the same to Steven when he comes back; you can't tell anyone. Let people find out for themselves, just like you did,' said Gary.

'Oh! You don't need to worry about that. Our lips are sealed,' replied Donna.

'Celebratory shots, anyone?' Steven put the Jägermeister and Red Bull shots, known as Jaeger bombs, on the table. 'Your secret is safe with us.'

It was as though he had been listening to their conversation.

'I just told him the exact same thing,'

'Great, that means we are all on the same page. Cheers to the next operation and bringing hell upon those who deserve it. Raise our glasses to Justice,' said Gary as they downed the Jaeger bombs.

Chapter 9

Hangovers were something neither of them was used to, but this was a special occasion. Donna was first to wake up, and she wanted to die quietly in bed. The beer fears perfectly described the rough feeling and horrible anxiety. She couldn't stay awake alone, so she woke Steven up.

'Leave me alone,' he murmured in a half sleepy voice as if he was in pain.

'Why did we do that?' Donna whispered in his ear.

'Because we are stupid as fuck.'

He turned to face Donna.

'Can we do nothing today?'

She snuggled up to Steven with her arms over his chest.

'What day is it?' Steven tried to sound jovial.

'It's still not tomorrow.'

Donna asked if breakfast would make them feel any better.

'I couldn't eat anything just now; the thought of it makes me feel sick. Whose idea was it to drink shots?'

The half-smile fell from his face as he saw Ben wagging his tail.

'Fuck! Ben needs out. The poor dog hasn't been out of a decent walk for hours,' Steven said, guiltily.

'Shall we take him out and see if a walk makes us feel any better? I'll take a quick shower, and then you can go in. We can walk to the park.'

Her lack of energy meant she struggled to get out of bed.

It was late morning, just after eleven. Certainly not the usual time to get up, but the night with Gary had almost killed them with the unusual amount of alcohol they consumed. Although feeling fragile, they got showered and walked to the park, where the only happiness around them was Ben.

As they were heading home from the park, Gary called.

'How are my two great drinking buddies feeling today?' he enquired.

'Rough as fuck, mate. It's a day for Netflix and the couch. I really can't function today,' Gary admitted.

'Grow a set of balls, the pair of you, and toughen the fuck up.' There was no sympathy in Gary's voice.

'It was a great night, but I can't justify the hangover to do this again; the fears are getting ridiculous the older I get,' said Steven.

'I'm going to be passing your place in an hour. Are you putting the kettle on?'

'Yes, that's not a problem; where are you now?'

'Just passing Talbot Road. I'm going to meet Chelsea for a coffee. Have you met her?'

'Never mind her just now; there are more important issues to resolve. Are you around that area before coming to mine? You could do me a huge favour.' Steven crossed his fingers.

'Yes, she stays about three minutes away.'

'OK, for me to make you tea, you need to bring two-foot-long steak and cheese, with extra cheese and bacon, on Italian herb bread from Subway.'

'Please, Gary!' Donna begged from the background.

'OK, not a problem. Toasted?'

'Yes, please, mate, you're a fucking superstar for doing it, lifesaver.'

'OK, I'll tell you what I'll do. I'll go meet with Chelsea, and we'll all get Subway and just head over to your place and have lunch together, so put that kettle on as soon as you get home; I won't be too long.' Gary ended the conversation.

The walk home to Steven's flat passed quickly. They picked up the pace, with the thought of tucking into a foot-long Subway. Ben had been running around the park chasing seagulls and returning sticks for almost an hour now. He would settle at home, having burned off some energy. For a second, Steven thought how lucky Ben was, as he could just go home and sleep.

The kettle boiled and, while Steven arranged the cups, he left two with no milk and sugar. He didn't know what his guests thought was the perfect cuppa. Donna had a quick tidy up around the flat before they arrived. Neither of them had met Chelsea before, and first impressions are things that lasted.

The ring of the doorbell announced their arrival.

'Good afternoon, Gary. How the hell are you looking so fresh?' Donna gave him a welcoming hug.

'I really don't know; I've never really suffered from hangovers, like ever,' said Gary as he turned towards Chelsea.

'You must be Chelsea.' Donna greeted the dark-haired woman standing behind Gary.

'Hi, Donna, nice to meet you.'

They walked into the living area where Gary had placed four cups of tea on the table, along with a small jug of milk and a bowl of sugar.

'Nice to meet you, Chelsea; welcome to my crib,' Steven said in a joking manner that implemented that he was a youngster still.

The food was gone in minutes, and they were now on their third cup of tea. No alcohol to be seen. Chelsea fitted right in with them. She was gorgeous. Around five foot eleven, with a slim body and long black hair. She wore little makeup and wasn't the type of woman who spent money getting her nails done every week. She was just naturally pretty. Donna saw why Gary was friends with her.

As the conversations carried on, they could see they could get on well with Chelsea. Gary had known her for six years, and they soon established that she was also involved with some online activism. Nothing on the same scale as Gary, but more than Steven or Donna.

'So, what's your moniker then, Chelsea?' asked Donna

Gary burst out laughing while looking at Chelsea.

'What's so funny? You leave her alone!' Donna cheekily ordered Gary.

Chelsea put her hands over her face, head down at the table top, avoiding eye contact with anyone.

'It's Midnight's Princess,' said Chelsea.

Her face went bright red. Steven laughed as Gary went to give her a hug.

'That's so cute,' said Donna, with a smile and puppy eyes.

'So, are you two a couple? You kept that a secret, lad. You sure are punching,' joked Steven.

Punching, as in punching above his weight. A nice compliment to Chelsea.

'We have been seeing each other on and off for almost four years, but someone lacks commitment, eh Gary?' Chelsea's tone couldn't disguise an element of truth.

'One day, Midnight's Princess,' Gary whispered as he kissed her on the forehead.

'We need to do something together, like a double date,' Donna suggested. 'Something really nice and relaxing.'

'Do you two like camping?' asked Gary.

'I've not been camping before,' Donna told them.

'I've not been for around ten years. Let's arrange it then. It will be fantastic. A few beers around an open fire in the middle of nowhere. Complete tranquillity.' Gary painted the scene.

'We don't have any camping gear, but I know my brother has a new tent and some accessories. I could borrow that, no problem,' Steven chipped in.

'I have just about everything you can imagine at home; we go camping but not as often as we would like. Don't worry about anything else. Get the tent and sleeping bags or blankets, and I will take care of the rest,' Gary added.

Gary and Chelsea stayed at Steven's flat longer than they imagined. It was almost dark outside when they left. They had a brilliant afternoon. Like great friends should do. The four of them spent time together and, now and again, Donna and Chelsea disappeared into the bedroom for some girl gossip. Donna showed her some clothes and old photos.

It amazed Steven that Gary had such a vast knowledge about computers, and he helped Steven tweak his laptop, upgraded his security to a program that Steven had never heard of, and gave him some free software that could come in useful another day. They agreed that camping couldn't wait. None of them had plans, so if they could arrange food and drink in the morning, they would set off the next afternoon.

'What's the weather like?' Donna asked as Steven stood at the window.

'It's like the perfect summer's day. A day for beer, shopping and tent borrowing,' laughed Steven.

They didn't waste any time going to the local supermarket. Donna chose easy to cook things plus water, juice, beer and cider. They picked up the tent from Steven's brother's house. Ryan was still in good shape and doing well from himself. Steven thought he should visit more often, and next time he wouldn't only go there to borrow something.

The tent was huge. It had a vast centre socialising area, big enough to park a car in. It had four compartments around the sides to make it an eight-man tent. Ryan also gave him an inflatable bed, an ideal size for one compartment. Their plans came together.

Gary started loading the car. He had everything, including another bed and a couple of inflatable two-seater couches. He threw in a fold-away table and small buckets with massive candles inside that promised to keep the flies away at night. That was a mere sales pitch; they only provided light.

Chelsea jammed the cool box between various items to prevent it from moving. It contained four bottles of wine and was topped up with a few bags of ice.

With both cars packed, it was time to meet up. As Steven wasn't familiar with their intended location, Gary suggested meeting at the petrol station on Hope Street, just before Asda, which was the last supermarket before they hit the country B roads, fifteen miles before the campsite.

'Hey guys,' Chelsea shouted from the passenger window of Gary's car.

'Who's excited?' asked Donna. 'I've brought the camera for lots of photos.'

'Let's get drunk again!' Gary suggested as he pulled out of the car park and nodded for Steven to follow his lead.

Traffic was really quiet on the back roads, so they arrived in next to no time. The scenery was amazing. They were in what they could only describe as a green valley. For three hundred and sixty degrees, they saw only substantial green hills. Animal farms were close by, but there were no animals in the fields and no sign of any farming activity. It was spectacular and only down the road from where they all lived.

'Why have I never been here before?' Donna asked in a disappointed voice.

Next to where they parked the cars was a small shallow stream, only deep enough to cover your ankles, but around twenty feet across.

'Come and see this?' Chelsea exhaled with excitement, wanting them to see another part of the stream.

'Oh, my fucking God,' said Donna as she got closer to the bend in the stream.

It was a postcard-perfect. The little stream had turned into a vast pool just one hundred yards away. It went from inches deep to around four feet in the deepest part, and at the furthest end of the pool, there was a waterfall of approximately eight feet.

'You'll hear this during the night, Donna,' said Chelsea. 'This place is amazing; how did you find it, with it being in the middle of nowhere?' asked Donna.

'My dad used to bring us here as kids. Me and sisters. We never camped back then. It would just be a barbecue and a swim during the summer. It's amazing, eh?' Chelsea replied as they walked back to the men who were busy putting up the tents.

Although it had been years since Steven had gone camping, he got Ryan's enormous tent up in next to no time. While the men saw to the tents, the women sorted the food and drink, arranged the bedding and blew up the mattresses.

It was now around seven in the evening. Only a couple of hours of daylight remained.

They all did their bit, collecting firewood until they had enough to last them the night.

'Who's hungry?' Steven asked as he lit the gas stove, which sat on Gary's one-and-a-half-metre fold-away metal table.

'I'm thirsty after all that hard graft,' said Gary.

He opened the cool box and threw Steven a beer.

'Do you ladies want me to pour you a wine?' Gary asked, just as they finished with the tents.

'White for us both, please,' replied Donna.

After food and a few beers, they were sitting around the fire. They weren't drunk but near to it. Oasis and Champagne Supernova blared from the chargeable Bluetooth speaker Gary had brought. It was a cosy atmosphere. As Gary was a regular camper and had gathered different equipment over the years, he placed lighting around the entire location. Red lights, blue lights, green lights; it looked pretty spectacular once the sun went down. The surrounding lighting and the fire created a romantic atmosphere.

'I'm really impressed, Gary.' Donna looked around. 'You have made this field look more than special. Thanks. I just love it,'

'You should do it more often. You really can't beat the great outdoors, especially here. Few people know about this location, so keep it to yourself!' Gary whispered.

'We should make this a regular thing, weather permitting.'

Steven took a swig of his beer.

'Yes, fuck coming up here in January,' joked Donna.

They added more wood to the fire; it was getting cold, but not January cold. Within minutes, they were warm again and moving back from the heat. The alcohol was taking over; they were one hundred percent under the influence.

They had switched off and enjoyed each other's company for a few hours. That was, until Gary had an issue. This was when the group chat returned.

'That arrogant bastard is having a visit from karma soon,' said Gary, straight out of the blue and changing the conversation.

'Who are you talking about?' Steven looked at the others.

'It's something I was working on a while ago, but because of circumstances, I never got around to it. Have you heard of Medicod UK, a pharmaceutical company that increased the price of cancer drugs in the UK and is costing the NHS hundreds of millions more every year? Colin Oscar-Douglas is the CEO, an arrogant bastard of a man,' said Gary while screwing up his face in anger.

'What were you working on? Were you working with a group?' Donna was curious.

'No, this was a solo project, a simple website takedown, and I left a message with a twenty-four-hour warning. That was a few weeks ago. The website is back up and running and the prick thinks he's getting away with it. Not a fucking chance!' Gary screamed at the top of his voice.

He created an echo across the dark valley, much to everyone's amusement.

Gary explained what he had done, about other things that happened, and how he was too tired to follow it up. After thinking it over a few days, he hadn't been sure if he should get the group involved.

Gary hated Colin so much that he felt violence was the answer, but that would only give his victim headlines. He needed something more, something embarrassing.

'Would any of you be interested in getting involved?' Gary surveyed the faces that were staring at him.

'What do you have in mind?' asked Chelsea.

'How big is the operation, and is it a funny one?' Donna laughed.

They weren't really concerned about public opinion because they were dealing with one of the UK's most hated men. They concluded that since people were dying, the best way to draw attention was to colour him, but what colour? And where?

'This has been an awesome night, but can we drop the group chat, please?'

'I agree with Chelsea. I have enjoyed tonight, but it's great to get away from the conversations about politics, groups, activism and just have fun,' said Donna.

'Who's good at karaoke?' asked Steven. 'Who's singing the first song?'

It was seven minutes to midnight, and they were drunk. There was a bit of a mess around the campsite, even though they had hooked a bin bag on a fence. They weren't worried. They were responsible and knew the country code. A quick clean-up and leaving the place the way they found it was inevitable.

Steven was the first to stand up and declare he'd had enough, and it was time for bed. There was no argument from the other three. Gary, who was probably the drunkest, got up from his inflatable couch and wished Steven and Donna goodnight. They all hugged in a group and left for their tents. Gary and Chelsea's tent was around thirty feet to their right, and Steven and Donna's tent was just on the bank of the small stream, in the opposite direction, about forty feet away.

'Are you really going to sleep?' Donna had a smile on her face.

'Not if you have other plans.' Steven looked into her eyes.

'We could still get ready for bed, but we don't have to go there. We could play quietly outdoors for a while,' Donna suggested.

Steven knew what she meant. Sex outdoors in the middle of nowhere. He could hardly hide his excitement and almost skipped to the tent to take his clothes off. And Donna wasn't far behind. Once stripped, they came out, making sure they were far away from the other tent. They walked further along the riverbank, in and out of the trees.

'Here is good enough,' said Donna, as she grabbed Steven by the neck and started kissing him in a fast-passionate way. She wanted sex and wanted it there and then.

Within minutes, they were both standing in the field, totally naked. Steven was placing hands all over her back and kissing her neck. Donna was scratching his back, and they were sharing one of their greatest moments together. Steven pushed her against a tree, and they had passionate sex. Donna was in heaven, as was Steven. It was their first time having sex outdoors. Donna turned around and placed her hands on the tree, and immediately Steven took her from behind. He held on to her blonde hair, giving it the odd pull, much to Donna's satisfaction. Then it was over.

They both fell to the ground and lay naked in each other's arms. Their sweaty bodies released steam into the countryside darkness. For a few minutes, they said nothing to each other. They were on the same page and wanted to enjoy their surroundings with each other in complete darkness and the openness of the great outdoors.

'That was out of this fucking world,' said Donna.

'Amazing! What you doing next weekend?'

They laughed.

'We need to do this more often; what the fuck have I been doing with my life?' Donna asked herself out loud. 'Your life has changed now, so has mine. I love being with you. I'm regretting not letting this happen years ago. So, we have lost time to make up for.'

They lay on the grass for a while, having some pillow talk with each other's arms for cushions. They would have stayed there all night, but the sweating eased and they felt the cold, so they cuddled and walked back to their tent for a decent night's sleep.

After Gary and Chelsea went to their tent, they too had passionate sex but, as Gary had consumed the most drink, their experience was in a much lower league from Steven and Donna.

Chapter 10

Once the camping trip was over, Steven and Donna spent as much time as possible together. They were in love for the first time. The days of being fuck buddies were gone. They stayed home watching movies during the day and were trying out restaurants that they had walked past hundreds of times but never thought of going in. Both had a glow about them. You could say they looked like the old TV advert from the 1980s for the breakfast cereal Ready Brek, where anyone who ate it had a glow all around their bodies. What they had between them was beautiful, and they knew it.

One day, Steven sat at home alone while Donna was doing her four-hour shift at the hotel. He had been catching up with the group, and it became apparent that they missed him when the welcome back message appeared on the chat logs.

He read the post about Colin Oscar-Douglas, created by Gary the day before. A lot of support was required for such an operation. The general opinion online was that the hacked website did little; it was completely ignored and never even made the media. It was now time to step things up a gear.

Gary met a couple of the group, and as usual, invited Steven and Donna. There was one condition, though. Nobody was to offer him an alcoholic beverage. Everyone replied to his post with many laughing emojis.

Donna's manager had mentioned to her earlier that morning how happy she looked recently, and it was great to see her getting on in life. She also told Donna the colleague that shared the job with her would leave at the end of the month and that she would offer more time to Donna if she wanted, taking her hours up to thirty-eight.

Steven met her at work, and to her surprise, he turned up just before she finished with a dozen red roses. She loved them and couldn't leave without showing them off to her colleagues.

'Thank you so much, honey. I love them; they are gorgeous!' She kissed him.

She then told Steven her good news.

'That's amazing; I'm thrilled for you, sweetheart, so you're not looking for another job now that you have more hours?' Steven asked.

'No, this will do me just right. The job's pretty decent; only the hours were the issue,' replied Donna.

'Celebratory drink?' he said, knowing all too well the answer would be a yes.

They headed down to what they now called their local, The Fox Bar. They had been there often enough to merit the title. Gary's car was already in the car park.

'How are you doing, mate?' Steven asked.

'Steven, mate, it feels like I haven't seen you in weeks. Hi Donna gorgeous, how are you?' enquired Gary.

'I'm buzzing about life today. My man brings me flowers, and I get the full-time hours at work from the end of the month; what's not to like?' replied Donna.

'You soppy big bastard, buying the missus flowers. What you after? A wee blowjob tonight, is it?' Gary screwed up his eyes as he and a couple of others laughed.

'I might take a leaf out of your book and buy some flowers on the way home,' Gary pretended to be deep in thought.

Steven had seen Gary's post online about no alcohol offers. He went to the bar knowing what Donna would drink, but took the chance to buy a pint of cider for Gary. His hands full, he walked towards Donna and the table.

'Here you go, mate. Grab one of them off me, will you?'

'I hope that's not for me?' Gary opened his eyes wide.

'Well, mate, you need to be clearer when posting. All you stated was that nobody was to offer you a drink. I didn't offer, I bought you one. So technically, you should just put your big boy pants on, say thank you and get drinking,' was Steven's reply.

'You're a sneaky, big bastard!' Gary grinned.

This meeting in the pub would not turn into a major drinking session. They needed to get themselves active again. It had been too long since the last stunt. After much discussion and avoiding the subject of kidnapping many times, much to everyone's amusement, they agreed they would target Colin Oscar-Douglas in person and fuck the victim card always played when things didn't go his way.

Only with an additional two people could they do the task. Brad and Andy would be there; the others had work and family commitments. Six was enough for the plan to go ahead. Some ideas involved Colin's family, but that would be the next step. Now they had a trick up their sleeves that would send a message that they were not bluffing.

Medicod's office was twenty-eight miles north of Castle Drum. The plan was to take two cars and wait. Colin only went to the headquarters once a week for a meeting, usually a Thursday afternoon. He wouldn't make it on a Monday because of a hangover; Tuesday and Wednesday, he spent time with the kids, and Friday morning would be the start of his weekend. He was lucky to be at the meeting for two hours and away again. Living his attention-seeking, millionaire lifestyle.

He was the father of two kids to his recently divorced ex-wife, who had taken around seven million pounds off him in a much-publicised court case. She swore that one day she would write a book about her marriage to what she described as someone who was fame-hungry.

Thursday arrived, and they waited at the side of the company car park. It wasn't difficult to miss his bright red Ferrari 812, only eighteen months old and a starting price of two hundred and fifty thousand pounds without extras. Nobody liked to show off more than this guy. He had all the money and toys he needed, but he still couldn't find a new woman, something the media printed with every story, as an added point after each major headline.

'There he is!' shouted Andy.

'Right, everyone, as soon as he leaves the car park, masks on,' instructed Gary.

Adrenalin was kicking in for all six of them. This was it. Could they make a difference, or would they be wasting their time?

'Showtime, baby,' said Steven, which sounded totally out of character.

They put their masks on as Colin pulled out of the car park. They expected him to put the accelerator to the floor when he got on the straight, but they had carefully thought this through. When he came out of the car park, Brad pulled out right in front of him, with Steven and Donna as passengers.

Colin blasted the horn, and they saw him shouting abuse at the car in front. He was too angry to notice two things. The three people in the car wore masks, and they had covered the registration plate with black tape. Gary pulled out and caught up behind Colin, who was now sandwiched between two of his abductors.

Bradley in the front car slowed down and eventually came to a complete stop in the middle of the road. He slipped the car into reverse and got as close as possible without hitting the Ferrari. Colin was shouting, but nobody paid much attention to what he said. By the time he made any attempts to reverse, Gary was as close to the car's rear as Bradley was to the front. Steven and Donna got out wearing masks and gloves. Gary, Chelsea, and Andy got out of the vehicle at the rear. Andy took over the driver's seat of Gary's car while Gary went to the car's boot. Simultaneously, all four approached the vehicle to a now terrified Colin.

'Please, take the car if that's what you want,' he shouted through the closed window.

'Shut the fuck up!' screamed Gary as they started pouring liquid from bright red fuel cans over the paintwork.

'Please, you don't have to do this. What do you want?' he yelled, becoming more terrified by the second, no doubt thinking that his life was about to end.

'Be quiet and let me explain; if I can't explain, I will need to set this car alight. Are you listening?' Gary asked through his mask.

'Yes, yes, tell me what you want.' Colin was shaking.

'Tomorrow morning, you will inform the media that you will make a U-turn on the last drug price increase and apologise. Tell the country you made a huge mistake,' said Gary, as Colin sat listening.

'Do you fucking understand?' shouted Donna.

'OK, yes. I get it, I will do it,' Colin answered, with the realisation that they would not torch his car.

'Listen carefully, Colin. We already gave you a warning when your website was hacked. Did you think we forgot? This is your second and final warning. See that liquid we have just poured over your car? It's only water, but next time it'll be petrol, and you will cook like a fucking chicken. Are you fucking listening to me? Look at me!' Gary shouted.

'Yes, yes, I'm listening,' a now terrified Colin said, trying to stop his shaking with his hands gripping the steering wheel.

'Now, for my next trick, this is very important, and you must pay attention because you can put people's lives in danger if you don't. Understand?' asked Gary.

'Yes, yes,'

Gary took six photos from his pocket.

'I'm going to show you masked people, but they are not important. What you need to pay attention to are the people in the background. OK, now this is the first.' He showed Colin a photo of someone with a scream mask on.

'Who is that in the background, Colin?' Gary pointed at the photo.

'Oh no! Please, that's my son. I will make the announcement tomorrow, I promise,' said a now tearful Colin.

Gary continued to show Colin the remaining five photographs. Every photo was of a masked person taking a selfie, but in the background of each was a member of Colin's family. The second was his daughter, the third was his older brother, the fourth was his younger brother, the fifth was his elderly mother on a shopping trip.

'We will come after you, Colin. If you report this to the police, bad things in your life will be multiplied more times that you can imagine. Do you have any idea who we are?'

'No, I don't.'

'We are Anonymous. We are legion. We do not forgive. We do not forget. Expect us,' Gary said in a pleasant, calm voice.

'Oh, my God. OK. I will do it, I promise. Can I go now? Please?' begged Colin.

At that moment, they ran to their cars and made for the roads, which avoided motorway cameras. The road ahead was straight. At least as far as they could see, Colin didn't move anywhere. Was he on the phone with the police? They thought. At least he didn't follow them, which was positive.

Both cars got on the back-country roads as soon as possible and the drivers put the foot to the floor. As soon as they came to the first quiet parking spot, both drivers got out of the car and ripped off the black tape that hid their registration plates. Gary dropped Steven and Donna off in the centre of Castle Drum to go for some food. Everyone else went their separate ways once back in the town. They locked the cars up in a garage until they had further information on whether Colin had gone to the police. It was now a waiting game.

'Are you going to have something different from lasagne today?' Steven asked Donna.

'Yes, I think so; it's not as good in here as in The Fox Bar.'

'Did you see the terror on his face?' Donna asked, as they sat in the Italian restaurant on Milford Road.

'Yes, he was afraid. For a split second, I kind of felt sorry for him, but then I remembered why we were doing this. He more than deserved it. Let's keep our fingers crossed it sinks in, and he does the U-turn in the morning.'

They had a lovely evening over dinner, both chose pizza and a glass of red wine. They changed the discussion from the task to themselves and discussed how happy they were than before, but how much more comfortable they had become in each other's company. Although something happened that Donna was not expecting.

'Move in with me full time?' Steven proposed. 'I really mean it. If we are going to do this, let's do it right. It's not like I have just met you; we go back most of our lives. Give up your flat and move into mine. You won't have any rent, because I don't. It will be a big help to you financially.'

'Are you serious? Do you really want a woman's hair all over your lovely apartment?' Donna laughed.

'It's better than dog hair!' Steven scoffed.

Donna got up from her seat and walked around the table. She kissed Steven on the lips.

'I would love to move in with you; I'm so excited about the future together.'

Donna made her way to the toilet, where she would shed a few tears of happiness in private.

The following day, back at Steven's flat, they woke up just after eight and Donna put the coffee on.

'Do you fancy a pleasant morning walk down the forest with Ben?'

'But the sun is up; you are aware of what happened the last time we met in a forest; people will see us,' Donna gave him a playful look.

Steven chuckled.

'Let's get a quick coffee instead of sitting around all morning and get going. The sun is out, so let's take advantage of it. It could piss down tomorrow.'

Within twenty minutes of getting out of bed, they had finished a coffee and left the flat with an excited Ben. Steven took the dog lead with his right and placed his left arm through Donna's right arm, making sure she was on the inside of the pavement. It was his way of being a gentleman. He never forgot his grandfather telling him he always made sure his grandmother walked on his left in the street when he was younger.

His grandfather told him she would be closest to his heart, and there was more chance of a mugger coming from the roadside than the inside of the pavement. Also, his grandmother would never get wet if cars passed by and splashed them because of puddles on the road. Although he admitted that it never happened, it was nice for the ladies to hear.

They sat in the forest on top of a fallen tree. The sun shone directly on their faces. Ben was running around chasing whatever scent he had picked up. The dog was loving life just as much as his owner. The forest was tranquil in the morning; peaceful, just like the camping, with a lot nicer scenery than the flat land of the park where they usually took Ben.

'Who's calling me?' Steven took his phone out of his pocket to silence a ringtone that sounded really loud in such a quiet environment.

'Gary! Good morning, mate,' said Steven.

'It's happened. It's not got the TV coverage yet, but it's on Sky and the BBC website as breaking news. We fucking did it, mate!' Gary shouted down the phone.

'Are you fucking serious? Hold on, I'll put the phone on loudspeaker so Donna can hear.'

'I'm deadly serious. The media treat this like someone has leaked it from his office, like Colin planned to do last week. This is a huge result and one that's got me thinking,' said an excited Gary.

'Woo, hoo!' Donna did a little dance.

'Gary, I'm out of the house at the moment. I'll make my way home for a look at the TV and call you when we know more.'

Colin had taken the warning on board less than nineteen hours after their stunt and made the U-turn.

This would save the NHS hundreds of millions per year and save many more lives. Now the NHS staff could make more straightforward decisions. This result was massive, and as someone had said to Steven before, 'If one man can change the world, it's Gary.'

They arrived back at the flat. One put the kettle on, and the other put the TV on. Changing the channel from FOX News US to Sky News UK. There it was, on the ticker scrolling across the bottom of the screen. *Medicod backtrack on the vital drug price increase.*

They sat on the couch waiting on an official statement but didn't need to wait too long as the presenter said, 'Coming up soon, we will discuss the reasons behind the Medicod U-turn with CEO Colin Oscar-Douglas. See you after the break.'

Donna and Steven moved from their slumped position on the couch to sitting on the edge. Both burst with excitement at what was about to happen. They looked each other in the eye and, with no communication, simultaneously lifted their hands and high-fived each other. The commercial break was lasting forever. Three minutes seemed like ten.

'Welcome,' said the presenter.

She continued to explain the enormous increase in the cost of cancer drugs, the entire story and that the CEO now regarded it as an error of judgement.

'We can go live and speak to CEO Colin Oscar-Douglas now. Good morning, Mr Oscar-Douglas; thanks for joining us. Why the increase in the first place and why a U-turn?' asked the female presenter.

Looking not quite his usual bubbly self and not as cocky, Colin said, 'We, as a company, made a huge mistake. I won't go into the details of why we put the increase in place, as that is now behind us. I can say that, moving forward, we will not only be U-turning on the price, but we will also implement a fourteen percent reduction on the original price before the U-turn.'

'Yeeeeeeeeh!' Steven shouted at the TV.

'Be quiet, let him finish?' Donna was paying close attention to every word.

'What made you change your mind? Was it a self-guilt or public opinion?' asked the presenter.

'It was a bit of both, really. I don't think I thought through the consequences and the strain it would put on our wonderful National Health Service. I was brought up on the NHS and was born in an NHS hospital, as were my kids. I have not always been in the lifestyle that I now enjoy. It was a terrible judgement on my behalf.'

'And public opinion, how did you see that?' asked the presenter.

'Let's put it bluntly. I had met a few public members, and let's say it was an uncomfortable and extremely heated discussion. They put across very valid points, so, in the end, they were right, and I was wrong.'

At that point, the presenter thanked him for the right choice and for joining them on Sky News.

'Because you thought we were going to roast you, you fucking slimy bastard!' Steven roared at the TV.

'This is fucking tremendous. This is why we do what we do,' said Donna, as she cuddled and kissed Steven.

It was a victory for the people. All six met at The Fox Bar and celebrated, but kept their voices down and pretended they were celebrating Andy's birthday. Steven thought back to the death of old Stanley, and they quietly raised their glasses to him in a toast. This is the result they wanted. Therefore, they did what they did. There was no stopping them after they realised their accomplishments. They had many plans, but they were no longer an online hacktivist group; they were serious activists.

Chapter 11

Nine days later, the most popular discussion on the forum was regarding Medicod. There were almost a quarter of a million comments from members, with the majority congratulating the team for their incredible efforts and suggesting ideas for the following missions. More people wanted to be involved, but that ship had already sailed.

The forum was buzzing like it was back at the time of the BBC car-park attacks, but Steven and Gary took time away from online. They decided there was no need to get people from all over the world involved when it was always going to be UK-based. The more people knew, the higher the chance of getting caught. They were careful online, but they didn't trust the people one hundred percent. Now that they are more like activists than hacktivists, it was better to decrease their group and move to a new, more localised and smaller group; one with around fifty members who lived in London or the surrounding areas. Gary showed Steven how to set up a new forum and what precautions they needed to take for security measures.

Steven was glad they were moving away from the large group for a few reasons. The first one was it primarily comprised hackers. Second, he could never get to know them all personally; he could do that with local activists. The third reason was that Anonymous was becoming more familiar with the leftist movement. He didn't want to be associated with the political left. He hated the extreme left and Antifa, who he considered lunatics, who had no sense of reality in life. As far as he was concerned, Anti-Fascists are the real fascists.

Steven felt their tactics could get more physical and dangerous, so the fewer people he knew online, the better. He always advised others to keep their circles small to have less bullshit to deal with. So, moving to another group was ideal; they had discussed it just before they got drunk on their camping trip.

Steven and Donna were still inseparable and got back into a routine. Donna started her additional hours, and she loved it. Steven made a few more appearances at the office and was getting used to daily life after such a long time off, but he was missing the involvement with Gary, who was too busy with other personal issues in his life. It was like they were slowly drifting apart when all they were supposed to do was keep a low profile for a few days. Steven had not spoken to Gary in almost seven days, and he had not logged in online for the same period.

Maybe I should call him, Steven thought to himself while tidying his desk after a day at the office.

The good thing about his job and Donna's extra hours was he could meet her at finishing time. The hotel was only around a four-minute walk from his office and they now finished at the same time, whereas before it had been lunchtime, mid-afternoon or tea time.

Steven walked along Dalton Road to the hotel and pulled his phone from his pocket to call her.

'Hi there, I have booked a room for tonight, and I don't think I'm going to make it. Can I just pop in tomorrow and pick up my refund?' Steven disguised his voice.

'I'm afraid that's not possible, sir. We don't issue refunds here, and as it's less than twenty-four hours, there is no refund policy. I can give you some advice for later tonight and the next time you call,' Donna answered, trying to keep a straight face.

'And what would that be?' Steven continued, but with a different disguised voice.

'First thing you can do, sir, is when you meet your lovely partner soon, ask her if she would like to go for a drink. Second, next time you call, switch off your caller ID, you idiot!' Donna waited.

'Aw fuck. My number was a giveaway then. But my accent was OK?' he laughed.

'Steven, the last four digits of your phone number are one, one, one, one. It's kind of hard not to recognise! As for your accent, which one were you talking about?' She told him she'd be another five minutes and hung up.

Steven stood outside the hotel, waiting. He sat people watching. It was an interesting pastime, and he wondered what these people passing by had on their minds. He never judged them; he just asked himself if they were happy. If life satisfied everyone, he would be happy.

Life is a journey, not a competition, he always thought.

'Hi gorgeous, have you heard from Chelsea at all?' He kissed Donna.

'Not for a while; the last I heard, she was going to Glasgow for a few days with Gary, but that was a week ago. What's the plan for us?'

'Do you fancy a steak?' asked Gary

'Sounds lovely. Do you want me to WhatsApp her?'

'No, I'll give Gary a call just now and see what he's doing.'

There was a steak restaurant nearby, but the best one was near Gary's flat. So Steven made the call.

'Hello, stranger! Where are you? Not heard from you for a while. Are you nearby?'

'Steven, mate, sorry I have not been in touch. I had some family issues back home. It was my grandmother. We thought she didn't have long to go, so I went back to Glasgow for a few days, but she's fine now, and I just arrived back last night. Where are you?'

'We are just heading to the Steakhouse; do you and Chelsea want to join us? We can go for a drink if you need time to get ready,' Steven suggested.

'Give me about forty minutes, and I'll meet you there. Table for four it is. I look forward to seeing you both. It will be good for my head.'

Steven and Donna decided it would be better to go directly to the Steakhouse rather than find somewhere nearby to have a drink. The choice of bars was not that impressive, and The Fox Bar was in the opposite direction. They had revamped the Steakhouse since they were last there almost a year before, back when they were fuck buddies.

The entrance was glamorous, with vast chandeliers lighting up each side of the lobby on the way to the restaurant. It certainly had had a makeover, that's for sure. They had tastefully furnished the small bar area with giant single leather chairs, something you would expect to see in an old mansion. The antique look suited the surroundings. The wall behind the bar must have reached twenty feet and was full of shelves with mirrors and various coloured lighting. It was a touch of old and modern and looked tremendous. The staff looked tidy and spotless. Their black uniforms had a touch of pink visible through their tops. A luxurious place to have a drink while waiting.

Almost an hour later, Gary and Chelsea arrived, although Gary had kept them updated about the delay. That was the guy he was. He was usually very punctual, so, felt it was always polite to inform people if he was to be late.

'Have you two been here since breakfast?' joked Gary.

'That's what I like about you, Gary,' Steven replied.

'What?'

'Fuck all!'

The waiter showed them to their table, and after the usual catching up, they ordered food. It was time to talk about the group and the way forward.

'I want out, if I'm honest. I've had enough,' said Gary.

'What the actual fuck?' Donna was in shock and looked at Steven.

'Are you fucking serious, mate?'

'Yes. I've been doing this for too long. I'm getting to the stage where I need something else in my life. Something that brings the excitement like we had with Colin. It's OK trying to make changes behind a computer, but you never actually get to see their faces, if you know what I mean,' explained Gary.

'So, you're not leaving us? Is that what you mean? We have only just got started.' Donna sounded disappointed.

'Fuck no! I mean the online stuff, the hacking, the teaching, the organising, the putting up with people letting me down. People ask for help and then become cunts about it when I refuse. These are people I don't even know. My life became more of a virtual world for too long. I'm thrilled that I have met you two. If I'm honest, you both have changed my life for the better. Chelsea will back me up. I have been out of the house more since I met you both than I had in the five months before I met you.'

Gary picked up his pint, waiting for someone to say something and shorten the pause that left his words hanging.

Steven took it all in and was relieved that Gary was not leaving them. He winked at Donna.

'It's a genuine pleasure to meet you too, mate. I can see us being mates for a long time. If Donna and I are honest, we have been out and drunk more since we became friends. But for a moment there, I thought you were giving it all up.'

'Life is extraordinary, isn't it?' Donna piped up.

'What do you mean, sweetheart?'

'Well, think about it. If Stanley hadn't died, we wouldn't be sitting here now. You met online as you wanted help to take down a government website, and Gary replied to it,' explained Donna.

'That's very true, Donna. We take paths in life, and I always wonder, if I had taken a different course in life, where would I be now?' It was Chelsea's turn.

'Life's little mysteries, eh?' Gary chipped in.

'We're here for a good time now, a long time, so let's enjoy.' Gary raised his glass.

The small chat about life and friendship continued until they finished their starters. All choosing the beef carpaccio. The food was presented on a plate so large they joked that it resembled a bus wheel trim.

During the main meal, the chat started, and this time, their talk had a more serious tone to it. They agreed they needed better organisation and planning. Until now, their involvement was spur of the moment, excluding the mattress stunt with the lazy MP. They had too many people willing to assist, but now it was all talk and no action.

'We need a full-time researcher,' said Gary. 'Someone who can find people's local drinking establishments, bowling clubs, golf clubs, where our target spends their spare time.'

'That's very true; that's our starting point after all.' Steven agreed.

'Chelsea and I can do that. I mean, if we need to go looking in places, what do you think, Chelsea? Drinking while working. Does it sound good to you?' Donna laughed.

'If I'm sincere, ladies, I would rather you take that kind of role. It's a lot safer, and we never know when things might get dangerous.' Steven held his breath, hoping that Donna would agree.

'We'll be fine, researching online with wine,' said Chelsea, to everyone's relief with her one line of unintentional poetry. As Donna was working more hours, it would be ideal for her to research at night. Two stunning, long-haired women are very low on the scale of being refused entry to any bar, so finding some shady journalist in some posh security-protected door would be much easier. It would be perfect for both the ladies to strengthen their friendship.

Gary told them they had to forget any plans from then on, and it was back to the drawing board. Every idea had to be put aside, and they would need to create a list of priority cases, which they all agreed would be top priority. They also decided on three subgroups to target. Newspaper journalists, TV stations, and MPs. They would never target the same subgroup twice. Next, they would limit the group to sixteen people, and entry would be by invitation only. Only people they knew could be trusted. Andy and Brad were two. Gary would take care of the recruitment, as he had a network of people with unique skill sets.

Andy and Brad had recently become good friends with Gary. He had met both of them in a bar a few years ago through a mutual friend and, although they didn't hang out with them often back then, their being together had become more common over the last few months. Both were massive lads and had been eight years in the army together, serving Queen and country. They were never far from each other. If you saw one without the other, the chances are they had just left each other or were about to meet up. Nobody dared fuck with them. They could and would fight anyone, but would never start it themselves. They were down-to-earth lads who just wanted to enjoy life after being through more than their share of Middle East tours, fighting for what they now believe to be illegal wars.

Andy and Brad were cousins who had lived in Castle Drum most of their lives. They knew of Steven but didn't really speak until Gary introduced them one day in the supermarket.

With his tattoos and short black hair, Andy spent a lot of his time in the gym. With his more extended than usual blonde hair, Brad wouldn't think twice about putting a sweatband over his hair and running for miles. It was common for him to run around fifteen miles, possibly three or four times a week, but this is where their differences ended. They had three tattoos the same, listened to the same music, and had developed a hate for the politicians in the country they once served.

They were both disgusted at the lack of support for ex-servicemen. Many soldiers were left dealing with their own mental health issues, and these days there were too many sleeping on the streets. They felt the government had let them down, as most help was through charities. It was down to political reasons that they both told Gary that they would be more than willing to get involved should there be any protests or things that needed to be sorted. Although they knew Gary, neither of them had a clue about Midnight Justice.

'Anyone for dessert?' Gary asked to the sound of negative groans and the answer of no, without actually saying no.

'I struggled with the main, nothing more for me. Thanks, I can't even drink anymore. As much as I love you guys, I'm actually getting excited about the couch and a movie; make that half of a movie, or maybe twenty minutes.' Steven joked.

'I'm the same mate. Shall we get the bill and a taxi? We can drop you off at home. But I want you both to think about everything we have discussed tonight and stick to the plan.'

'Where's my boy?' Steven greeted Ben the minute the door was opened. He loved the dog, but it was not a night for walks. The heavens had opened, and the rain was bouncing off the ground; even Ben agreed when he was let out in the back garden and then returned within minutes. Within those few minutes, Donna had made tea and was sitting on the couch with a blanket. It was definitely a night for the house and doing nothing.

'Gary is right in what he said tonight. The organisation is the key,' said Donna.

'Yes, and you have been promoted to the chief researcher in a dual role with Chelsea.'

Over dinner, Gary had given them three names. One MP, one journalist, and one TV boss. All were a priority for different reasons. Gary had been eager when they discussed the MP, so bets were on this happening. Although it wouldn't happen until the trusted team was in place, they had a plan that wouldn't fail. This was going to be a very public and dangerous task, but that's what they wanted now. They were new-born activists that no one had heard of. They didn't even have a name yet.

Chapter 12

Less than three weeks had passed. The foursome met up pretty regularly, and developed a great relationship and social life, a life that Steven and Donna had missed for most of their adult lives. They were having lots of fun, mostly in restaurants and bars; they felt too old for clubs these days, which they found out one Friday night when the four of them consumed too much and thought it was a good idea to visit a nightclub. They went to the most famous one called Infinity. Never thinking about their age, they entered the club full of eighteen to twenty years old. All had a great night despite them feeling out of fashion.

Gary had a plan, and they discussed it at length. They decided an MP would be targeted, which made Steven animated. He had often read about David Johnstone, the MP for the nearby Summerhill constituency. There always seemed to be an article about him in certain newspapers; other tabloids completely ignored it. It was expenses or fraud, but there were never any consequence. It was the typical public apology and then move on to the next story. He also had shares in the pharmaceutical company owned by Colin Oscar-Douglas. And he failed to carry out any of his promises, which had got him voted in by his constituency. He was a tall, skinny, suit-wearing prick. Not as smug as his friend Colin, but cocky enough to be disliked by many. At fifty-four years old and an MP for over twenty years, David Johnstone knew the UK system and played it well.

'Today's the days we get that bastard,' Gary told Chelsea.

'Yes, the media are going to love this,' she replied while sitting on her fifties style bedroom bench, brushing her hair in her eight-light bulb lit mirror, four on each side.

'I'm happy; this has been coming for a long time.'

'I mean, robbing a charity is as low as it gets; the man is a snake!' Chelsea reminded him.

'He doesn't know what's coming,' scoffed Gary.

'OK, let's do it. Let's go and pick up Steven and Donna,' Chelsea suggested.

It was a Monday morning. The sun was just coming up, and the birds were singing. It was a beautiful day for what was about to happen. Steven had decided that he would take the next three days off work, and Donna worked the weekend, so she had the next two days off. They were wide awake around five-thirty that morning and had managed little sleep because of their nervousness and excitement.

'Gary will be here in ten minutes,' Steven shouted to Donna, who was sitting on a round stool in front of the mirror in the bedroom doing her hair.

'Grab the bag. Everything we need is packed. It's in the kitchen,' Donna shouted back.

Steven picked up the rucksack and checked everything that he needed was there. As he studied the contents, he ran through the process in his head. He accounted for everything. While waiting for Donna, he stood ready behind the front door, stretching and thinking of the day ahead. He thought back to the other things they had carried out and took his confidence from their success and the fact that no one suspected or caught him. Donna appeared from the bedroom. They looked at each other and smiled.

'Ready!'

'Let's do this,' she replied.

According to google maps, David Johnstone's office was around seventeen minutes' drive away. They knew he was there every Monday morning for a short while before he took the train into Westminster. Summerhill Station was only around four minutes' walk from his office, so he would leave his car in the car park. Not for environmental reasons, more of it was quicker, and he could drink afterwards. Everyone would think he was responsible when he took the train home later in the evening.

For four years, David had been the treasurer in I Need Help Brother, a mental health charity for men. A few months ago, a committee member exposed him for having spent seventy-four thousand pounds on things for personal use. These included tickets for him and his wife to Milan for the weekend, staying in a five-star hotel and a bar bill of just under five hundred and thirty euros. He didn't deny that he spent the money. He told the media the other committee members were aware of the trip, and it was for research into how Italy coped with men and mental health issues. Although he came back with no report, they soon discovered that no such event existed. There were no other committee members who agreed with him. They reported the theft to the police, but failed to press charges, even though he had committed a crime.

Gary and Chelsea picked Steven and Donna up at the time they arranged. Not a minute earlier, not a minute later. As they drove towards the Summerhill area, there wasn't much conversation. Nerves were kicking in. Fear, anxiety and adrenaline arrived simultaneously while listening to further political scandal on LBC on the car radio.

'We need to find a parking space somewhere around here,' Gary reminded them, as the fifteen-minute journey was ending.

'Where are Andy and Bradley?' asked Donna.

'They should already be there,' Gary answered. 'Everyone knows what they are doing?'

'We got this.' Steven's voice was animated.

He took various items from the rucksack.

'Stick to the plan, remember, and it will all be over in minutes.' Chelsea reassured the others.

In his office, David Johnstone stood up and put his suit jacket on. Designer suit. Nothing but the best. The cost was the equivalent of around six months' job seekers allowance, which was paid to the unemployed. He said his goodbyes to the two staff members and headed to the station. It was a routine he had carried out for many years. Walk across Talbot Road and stop at Costa Coffee for his tall, caramel latte and a slice of carrot cake. He would eat the cake on the premises and continue walking with the coffee. A traditional Monday sugar fix.

The street was busy; it always was. Cars tailed back at the worst traffic lights in the town. They seemed on green for a maximum of twelve seconds for vehicles heading towards the centre in the city. There were also hundreds of pedestrians around from early morning till late evening, going about their business. It was a day that many of them wouldn't forget in a hurry and it would mentally scar them, but they would also see the funny side once they knew the complete story.

David crossed over the last road and, around thirty feet from the station entrance, he noticed two men walking towards him. They were wearing clown masks and pretending to fight by punching each other on the shoulder and throwing weak punches. He put his head down and attempted to avoid eye contact. They looked crazy and dressed as though they were from the housing estates. As he passed them, they turned around and placed their arms inter-linked with David's.

'What the fuck are you doing?' he asked.

'Say nothing and keep walking. We have people that need to have a word with you. You have been a naughty boy, but I will say this; you clearly have nothing to worry about; nothing will endanger your life,' said Bradley.

'But if you want to continue your day without physical harm, move along with us and keep quiet,' Andy added.

David didn't have a choice. He looked around for police presence, but none was to be seen. This was karma, as David had also voted for police cuts. He knew there was no good in crying for help towards the public, as in society these days, people would walk past and mind their own business, taking the preferred option of not getting involved.

'What do you want? Who are you? Why are you wearing masks if I have nothing to worry about? I'm calling the police,' said a now agitated David.

'What? On this?' Bradley held up the phone that he had removed from David's pocket.

'Almost there,' Andy informed David.

They arrived at a junction, and before the traffic lights, they pulled David to one side and took him up an alleyway.

'Where the fuck are you taking me?' he asked, attempting to pull back to go in the opposite direction.

'Your destination is thirty seconds away; keep calm.' Andy whispered.

In the narrow alleyway were giant industrial-sized bins outside back doors of local shops. They had to be vigilant. Anyone putting the bins out would obviously see what was going on and possibly alert the police. Their plan was to count three minutes if they thought they had been spotted and then abandon the operation. The others were waiting hidden in a doorway halfway down the alley.

Andy spoke. 'We've reached our destination. Stand against that wall.'

Steven, Donna, Gary and Chelsea appeared wearing black coveralls, black shoes and their chosen clown masks. They walked the ten steps towards David.

'Well, well, David, you have been a naughty boy, eh?' Gary started.

'Who are you people? What do you want? Is it money? Take my wallet,' said a now terrified David.

'We don't want your money, David. We want justice.'
Steven was the spokesperson. 'We won't beat you up, so
don't worry, we just need to deliver a message.'

'What kind of message?'

'You see, David, we have an issue with a missing seventy
grand that you stole,' Chelsea said in a slow, calming voice
close to his right ear, as she began taking his suit jacket off.

'We know all about you, David, everything, about your
family, your mother and father, where you drink. We even
know you're a fan of Mr Singh's Indian restaurant, where
you go most Saturdays,' Donna told him.

'What do you want from me? What do you want me to do?
What message? Who is the message for?' David rambled on,
not understanding yet that the message was for him.

'Take your shoes off,' Gary instructed in a louder voice.

'Get them off and do what the fuck you are told,' Steven
continued in a threatening voice.

Donna pulled five-millimetre-thick white cable ties from
her rucksack. She clicked one into a loop and then joined it
to another, sliding it up her arms. Then she passed a cable
tie to Chelsea.

'What the fuck are they for? You told me I wouldn't come
to any harm!'

'No harm is coming to you; we promise you that,' Gary
shook his head.

'You are getting stripped to your underwear, though.'
Donna laughed.

'Yes, get that belt undone, or I'll cut it off.' Chelsea
followed Donna's lead.

'OK, OK, I will do what you want.'

Andy and Bradley watched both ends of the alleyway for movement or witnesses, maintaining a bit of distance away from the others. Neither wanted evidence on their clothes; they didn't have coveralls. David was now standing against the wall, shaking and shivering and surrounded by the two couples. Donna pulled two fluorescent pink hair dye cans from her rucksack and threw one at Chelsea. Steven and Gary took a few steps back.

'Spray this robbing bastard,' said Gary excitedly.

'Close your eyes and be a good boy,' said Chelsea, shaking the can.

David was doing everything he was told and complied with every instruction. Donna placed a small strip of paper over his eyes, and Chelsea began spraying his head and face.

'That wasn't too bad now, was it?' said Donna.

The others laughed as she removed the paper.

'Davie Barbie,' Steven mocked as Donna and Chelsea continued to spray the rest of his body bright pink.

David looked ridiculous; he was almost glowing, standing in an alley in only his underwear and socks, covered from head to toe in pink. It was hysterical to Gary and Steven, who stood watching. Now that the painting part was over, Donna bent down and placed the hooped cable tie over his foot, while Chelsea did the other foot and fastened the connection tighter around his ankle, with another hoop hanging.

'What is this for? What are you doing?'

'You'll see. Your humiliation is not over yet,' Gary explained.

Donna and Chelsea also placed cable ties on his wrists and again left another loop hanging from his body. It was time they faced the riskiest part; putting David back on the main street without being identified. Andy stood at the end of the alley and waited for a gap in the people who were passing. It was busy, but there would be moments. Gary waited on the green light from Andy before taking David into full public view.

'Almost time, David. Your fifteen minutes of fame have arrived. People might know who you are around here, but by tonight, you'll be known across the world.'

'You're going to place me on the main street like this, right?'

'Correct! You deserve it. You are low life scum, and we, the people, are fed up with your kind. It's time we fought back!' Gary spoke in an angrier tone.

It was time. Andy gave the green light. Gary and Steven grabbed David by the arms and walked him to the end of the alley.

'It's your time to shine,' said Gary as they entered David's public arena.

Donna ran towards the fence at the edge of the road, standing by with more cable ties in her hand. David was going along and still doing what he was told. He had accepted his fate.

'Up against the fence, Davie,' said Gary.

Donna and Chelsea grabbed the looped cable tie attached to the one tightly on his wrist. Donna pulled out another four cable ties and passed two to Chelsea.

They stretched David's arms out as far as possible and fastened the ties together, holding David to the fence. Then they tied his ankles and made him stand with all fours, spread like a human diagram.

'Where's the note?' Gary asked Chelsea.

'It's in my pocket. Don't panic.'

Chelsea pulled it from her pocket, unfolded it and put it directly in the face of David. 'This is what people need to know,' she retorted.

She placed the note on David's chest as Donna started pulling some industrial strength super sticky tape from the roll she took from her rucksack. The paint might come off easily, but duct tape would take every bit of body hair with it. They intentionally went over the top and used excessive tape. Bradley and Andy looked at Gary and nodded down the street to the south. It looked like a bus had stopped and people were walking in their direction. It was time to move. They had carried out the job exactly as they planned.

David stood, head bowed, and hoped for help. People were heading in his direction, but if anyone read the note, they would either take out their smartphone camera and create a video for social media or walk by.

They all headed back down the alley to the far-away end and took off their coveralls and masks, placing them in their rucksacks. It was time to get out of town as soon as possible. Back at the car, they congratulated each other on a successful operation.

Andy and Bradley doubled back and returned to the scene. They would keep their distance and watch from the other side of the road. The only way anyone would recognise them would be by their clothes, but there was nothing that stood out. Their black jackets, jeans and baseball caps were a disguise of sorts.

People approached David and saw the note on his chest. A few walked past laughing, some straight-faced and others shaking their heads in disgust. One person stopped and approached David.

'This is the least you deserve, you low life scumbag,' he shouted after reading the paper taped to his chest, which stated: *I'm your local MP, and I stole seventy thousand from a men's mental health charity*. In smaller letters, at the bottom of the page, it read – *Action carried out by The People for The People.*

David became more afraid. Although he was aware people would just walk on past, he never thought about the abuse he would receive. They tied him to a fence where he was totally defenceless. As the small section of the pavement got busier, people began laughing and taking out their phones. This was precisely what the group had hoped for. The last thing they wanted was, within minutes, someone cutting him free. He was now the centre of attention in a half-circle of people.

'Can anyone help free me?' David asked, to cues of laughter. They had humiliated him in his own constituency. Many people had heard of the fraud, but this would make sure everyone knew.

'Let me through,' said a voice from the back of the public circle. A small man in his seventies pushed his way between the crowd and placed a jacket over David's shoulders.

'Let's get you off here,' said the elderly gentleman.

'That would be much appreciated,' replied David, as the man went into his pocket and pulled out keys attached to his jeans by a short chain.

'I have a small pocket knife here; I will cut you free.'

He knelt down and cut the two ties from his ankles to *boos* from some of the younger crowd.

'Don't think for a minute that I have any sympathy for you,' said the man.

'I have been standing here for five minutes and think that you have gone through enough. You really deserve this, David. Maybe you'll think about your actions and the effects of how many men you denied mental health help to since the charity went under,' he continued while cutting off the straps that held his arms to the fence.

'Thank you for helping me. I understand your opinion, and I admit I made a huge mistake. My clothes are down that ally, I need to go down there.'

'Let him through. Move!' shouted the elderly man to the growing crowd. The number of people had multiplied, most of them with their phones in the air.

David went down the alley and saw his clothes lying exactly where they had stripped him. He gave them a wipe and got dressed while shaking uncontrollably, traumatised and becoming emotional. Instead of heading to the opposite end of the alleyway, he stupidly returned to the crowd, where everyone started jeering and booing.

Chants included, 'Lock-him-up, lock-him-up!' from everyone, laughing at his expense. He made his way back down the street in the same direction he came from and had to bear many strange looks. In a state of panic, he walked back to his office to call the police and shower.

After David returned from the alley, Andy and Bradley decided it would be better to cross over the road and capture some video footage themselves. There was not a chance anyone would recognise them in the crowd. They grabbed some good footage of David coming out of the alley and the public's comments, which ranged from:

'How the fuck is he still in a job?'

'Deserves everything that happened to him.'

'Karma is knocking, you thieving bastard!'

The public were angry, and who could blame them? One person commented that if he could rob a charity, then what else is he doing as an MP? MP's credibility was at an all-time low. Many were claiming for stupid things they had no right to do, which varied from house refurbishments just before they rented them out. It was a national disgrace. The tipping point was when one Tory MP claimed sixteen hundred pounds for a floating duck house, and it was then revealed he claimed around three thousand in gardening expenses over three years. People had zero sympathies for David.

He arrived back at his office building and went directly to his office, avoiding eye contact with everyone in his path. He sat for a few minutes and thought about calling the police.

'We know everything about you, David.' He remembered one girl saying.

If he went to the police, then maybe something else would happen on another day. David wanted to move on. He didn't want to be looking over his shoulders indefinitely. So, the MP took the option of heading to the adjoining room with a shower. He stood under hot water and had some shower thoughts. Once the videos appeared on social media, he told himself, life wouldn't be the same again. He had to do the right thing. The vigilantes would win, but it would make life easier for him and his family. He also thought of many what-if scenarios. What if they appeared at his home? The supermarket? Approached his wife? Anything was possible in his mind. It is a human instinct to think the worst because we all overthink scenarios.

'I need to repair this,' David thought to himself after one of the most prolonged showers he had ever taken. He looked at himself in the mirror, and the pink was gone. He was back to his usual tanned-looking self. It was at this moment his wife called.

'I saw what happened. Are you OK, darling?' she asked?

'How do you know? Let me guess? Social media?'

She acknowledged it was all over Facebook, and that a friend had sent her a link a few minutes before.

'I need to fix this, and the only way to do it is to set up a mental health charity. I provide funding only and let others run it. I'm fine. I had a bit of a fright, but I'm OK now, darling.'

He also informed his wife he would take the rest of the day off and be home soon.

Steven was buzzing. He had heard enough about David that made him genuinely hate the MP, and to carry out such a stunt made his day. He felt a sense of achievement. It had delighted all four of them, and of course, it was cause for celebration.

They had a double reason to celebrate. Not only did the six people carry out the stunt, but it was also the first as a new group. At their last dinner out, they agreed to the name TPFTP. They would gain public support with such a name, but only, as initially planned from day one, if nobody was physically hurt. They also discussed how far they had come from that first meeting, a day that seemed so long ago. Although they still spent hours online in the forum; it was time to deny any knowledge of this latest stunt, and through time they would remove themselves from the group altogether. Only six people to date knew.

Back at Gary's flat, they grabbed a can of cider each.

'A toast to The People for The People,' Gary said, as they raised their cans high for good luck and to the future success of their newly formed activist group.

Chapter 13

Social media was on fire. Facebook, YouTube, Twitter and Instagram. David Johnstone was everywhere; he had become more famous than he ever imagined. BBC, ITV, Sky News, Fox News in the US and Russia Today all covered the story, among other stations and newspapers. It had gone viral across the globe.

When people shared the video of an MP being humiliated, other videos from other countries became viral. Some were old, like when Ukrainians placed corrupt politicians in large industrial bins. People had a great laugh at their expense. TP4TP did it well, and they were proud of it.

Since the stunt, Steven and Donna had gone about their daily lives for a couple of days, while Gary and Chelsea carried out their planned decoration of Gary's flat. They didn't call each other and agreed to wait a few days before meeting again. The day arrived for them to catch up and go over the results of what they had accomplished.

'What are you doing?' Steven asked Gary.

'Just putting the finishing touches to the flat. It was a ball-buster. I fucking hate painting, especially the glossing. I'm not cut out for it. What are you two up to?'

'Thinking of lunch at The Fox Bar if you two can make it?'

'Will alcohol be consumed?' asked Gary.

'Does Burger King sell burgers?'

'OK. It's match abandoned here; I'll continue later. We'll grab a shower and be there in an hour. Quarter past one, good?'

With the time and place sorted, Steven was up for more than a couple of beers. He was in party mode. His last couple of ciders at Gary's place were exactly that. That had been his last drink. They had run out of alcohol but decided against going to the shop for more, so today was the day. He loved an afternoon drinking session, but first, he had to take Ben for a walk so that he could sit in the pub with less of a guilty feeling that he might neglect Ben.

As they walked to the park to throw a couple of tennis balls for the dog, Donna turned and grabbed Steven's arm.

'Look at that, that is just beautiful!'

A golden Rolls Royce slowly drove past with a smiling bride in the back.

'That will be me one day.' She laughed, but dropped a hint.

'If we get married one day, I know a guy who has a black car that would get you to the church on time for cheaper. Although we would have to cover up the yellow light on the roof!' Steven was referring to a black London taxi.

'Don't you even think about proposing, if that's your idea!' Donna pushed him away.

It was then, for the first time, Steven thought about marriage, but he saw it had animated Donna.

They spent the next forty minutes entertaining Ben by playing fetch. Where did he get the energy from? He wouldn't give up. It was time to drop Ben off and head to The Fox Bar. Steven chased Ben, who still thought they were playing a game. Ben didn't realise the importance of cider, schedules and times. They would now be late for the quarter past meeting.

Steven dropped Ben at the flat and, as he left, he saw the sadness in the dog's eyes. Even after the walk and play, Steven felt guilty. After all, Ben had been his only family for a long time. He called a taxi.

'What time do you call this?' Gary asked as Steven and Donna got out of the taxi.

'Dog troubles mate,' replied Steven

'What have you done, Donna?' Gary joked.

'Shut up! You're a cheeky bastard! Get the round in.'

'We've just arrived two minutes in front of you; we met Andy on the way down. He'll be here in about an hour and will give Brad a call soon,' said Gary.

They made their way into The Fox Bar and ordered the usual. Now it was time to share information from the David Johnstone operation. Steven started off with the news that everyone was aware of, but they felt the need to discuss the excitement that followed, even it if meant repeating themselves.

David Johnstone had spent the previous morning on various breakfast TV shows with his wife and explained his reason for standing down as an MP. He also said that they both planned to set up a new mental health charity, and they would hand it over to people who are best suited for the job. They would also invest ninety-five thousand to get the project off the ground, and it would be based in one of David's offices.

The TV hosts didn't give him a peaceful time, even though he had made a complete U-turn from his previous behaviour. Despite various interviews, it was on Channel Five he made the most impact by telling the audience about the message he received via Twitter the night before the show.

The message had been from a woman named Christine from Watford and had a real impact on him. She was calm in writing, and at no point did she ever get cheeky or abusive. She simply let David know that her twenty-nine-year-old brother was attending the charity he had robbed and was making significant progress. Christine was seeing her brother return to his usual self after mixing with people who understood him. She also stated that the charity was doing a tremendous job until it folded, and two weeks later, her brother took his own life. This hit David hard. He had failed to realise the consequences of his actions, and his selfish, money-obsessed lifestyle blinded him. His wife was by his side, which was very unusual for any MP's TV interview. She told how he broke down the night before they went in front of the cameras. She was as honest as anyone could be, and her body language and voice said she was sincere in every word. If not, they should nominate her for a BAFTA for her performance.

Steven and Gary discussed the outcome further while the women spoke about women's things, home furnishings and fashionable decorating styles. Gary put his hand out to Steven and shook it firmly.

'This was us, mate. We made this happen. It's about finding the right measures and people's weaknesses,' said Gary.

'We can do so much more if we keep the group small and not tell a single soul.'

'It's the way ahead, but I think we need to wait, and our next target needs to be a journalist, especially after their approach to reporting David Johnstone's story. While it was a happy ending for him and us, by the looks of it, the media bastards made him look the victim when he deserved every emotion he suffered.' Gary picked up his pint.

Sky News were the worst offenders. Their afternoon female presenter had her head so far up her ass, she could see her tonsils. A full-time egotist, who, if she was chocolate, she would eat herself. A presenter who asks the most stupid questions loses her professionalism when given a foolish answer. How she remained at a job is anyone's guess. Her reaction to the David Johnstone case was ridiculous. She totally forgot why it happened in the first place and not once was it mentioned. Although she was only doing her job, her producers were whispering instructions in her ear, making her a target would cross the line. They decided between them, they wanted the editor. The man ignored the authentic stories and chose celebrity bullshit over real global issues.

Mathew Vincent was a lanky scaffolding pole. His legs must have measured around six feet, with some exaggeration. People said how thin he was and very unhealthy, but he was just naturally like that and he wasn't shy of a few pies come lunchtime in the canteen. He could undoubtedly eat, and it amazed others at Sky that he gained little weight, especially when he swallowed a dessert every day, sometimes twice per day.

People nicknamed him beanpole with his dark hair and strange-looking face; he resembled Mr Bean slightly. The same hairstyle as the comedian didn't do him any favours. He had worked at Sky for over thirty-seven years in various positions, joining after many years at Channel Four, when it first launched in nineteen eighty-two. He was a cameraman back then on the news, so he had been in the industry longer than most. At age sixty-two, he had met many famous people in his day, from pop stars and movie stars to politicians. He had a total dislike for the Conservative party and bordered on the extreme left.

'Who loved Twitter on our famous day?' asked Gary, interrupting the women talking about wallpaper.

'It was on fire,' replied Donna. 'I fucking loved it!'

'It was trending in London in eighth place for around an hour with the hashtag #PinkJohnstonefraudster and just #DavidJohnstoneExposed.' Chelsea informed them.

'I was just saying to Steven that this was another successful operation, and you two played a blinder. We are slowly making a difference. Small, but still a difference.' Gary looked Donna in the eyes.

'We'll take our time and plan the next one, but Gary and I think we should go after the Sky News editor, Mathew Vincent,' said Steven.

Andy and Brad walked through the door of The Fox Bar. They walked up to the others to greet them as though they had not seen one another for months; all smiles and bursting with excitement again.

'I have our next target in mind. An evil, self-loathing, egotistic, ungrateful bastard,' said an angry-looking Andy, knowing that he didn't really get to call the shots but putting the idea out there.

'Calm down, mate. What's the issue here? Who is he? Share with the rest of us.' Gary had a look of interest and curiosity.

'The editor of the Sun. He's a total prick, Gary,' Andy explained. 'Last night online, I found the number of lies this newspaper has printed over the years, all on one huge file. It's fucking outrageous. How do they get away with destroying people's lives?'

Unknown to the others, Andy's niece had taken her own life only eleven weeks before and after the Sun newspaper printed a picture of her outside the town court and accused her of having links with the terrorist group ISIS. They questioned her chances of running off to Syria. The name reported in the paper was not her name, but it included a picture of her walking past the court on her way to work. She had no links and was only going about her daily routine. It was a case of mistaken identity.

People saw the name as incorrect; others paid little attention to anything other than the photo. Her name was plastered all over Facebook and Twitter, with a comment attached implying that the Sun had got the name wrong, but this was the right person. It was that day they turned her life upside down. She couldn't take the death threats, being called a traitor, the cyberbullying and the hate mail once her address was exposed. Her family contacted the

Sun, and they printed an apology two days later, with zero compensation offered. Still, the damage was already done, and the original article had gone viral in many countries outside the UK.

Andy was heartbroken and took it upon himself to take on the Sun by digging up as much evidence as possible. This included journalists' names and addresses. He had become a one-man army or spy, and only in The Fox Bar that day did anyone else get to know of the extent and research he had carried out.

The others sat speechless for the next fifteen minutes at Andy's story.

'You have all the details already?' asked Gary.

'Yes, I have been on this for seven weeks now. I know where they drink, what time they leave the office. Pick a journalist from the Sun, and I will tell you about them.'

'I just googled the Sun, and the first to appear is a story from Angela Nixon,' said Chelsea.

'Angela Nixon. Aged forty-eight, has never been married and has no children. She has worked at that rag for four years and has been in journalism all her life. She likes a drink, mostly champagne in The Lock Bar, three nights a week at least, and has dreams of becoming famous. Stays at number four Milton Gardens in a three-bedroom detached house alone. She owns a stupid little dog, but I'm not sure of the breed!' Andy ranted without taking much of a breath until he finished.

'Fucking impressive, mate. You have done your homework,' Steven commented.

'My desktop is full of information regarding these cunts. What do you think? Can you guys help me?' He appeared to get a little emotional with the only tear getting wiped away before anyone could really notice.

Gary took a deep breath, and they shared a long pause. This surprised them, and they needed to take in what had just been said. This was supposed to be a celebration drink, not a planning event.

'We had a slight mention earlier about our next target, but nothing serious or confirmed yet. I think if one of our own needs help, it should take priority.' Donna showed compassion for Andy.

'I one hundred percent agree, Donna,' said Chelsea.

'I agree; why didn't you tell anyone before now?' asked Gary.

'I felt it was my battle and didn't want to get anyone else involved. If you had seen me a few weeks ago, I could have murdered someone from the Sun, but I have taken my angry glasses off and think with you guys we can do it the right way.'

The women got up, gave Andy a hug, and told him they were all in this together. They had deep sympathy for him, losing a family member to these bastards. It was true, though. The UK mainstream media lived in a world of their own and there were minor consequences when they did wrong. It's a printed apology on page seventeen somewhere at the bottom of the page and minimal compensation to the victims. They needed to be brought back to earth, and this time they were more serious than ever before. It was one of their own this time.

'How should we approach this?' asked Gary.

'I think this time the petrol cans should have petrol in them. Let's blaze a car for a change,' Gary proposed. 'The last time, it was just water, but this time a life has been lost, and these bastards deserve some kind of real-life threatening attack.'

'I will happily pour it over the car,' Andy replied.

'Who is the target though?' Brad had said little until this point.

'Let's target a family member of the editor. Do you have info on him?' Gary asked Andy.

'Raymond Park-Smith, aged sixty-one,' replied Andy before he was interrupted.

'Another one of them fucking double-barrelled surnames,' Steven scoffed.

'He has three adult children. One daughter and two sons. I hear the sons don't live in England anymore, but I can't be certain. His daughter is Christine McDonald, who lives with her Scottish husband and two kids about twenty miles from Castle Drum.'.

'How do you know that?' Chelsea asked Andy.

'I followed her home from his house to hers one night. I had to hold myself back. I really wanted to beat her husband up for the sake of it, but she had the kids in the car.'

'Fuck me, mate. You really have been about!' Steven took another gulp of cider.

'She's the one. Let's make sure she gets the message that it's all her father's doing. Then we go for the prize itself a few days later.' Gary suggested.

'I also followed her to work one day after she dropped the kids at school,' said Andy.

'Where does she work?'

'She runs her own travel agency in Darington, which is not too far away. She's there five days a week,' said Andy.

The group continued drinking and, after an hour, they dropped the conversation when Gary suggested they enjoy themselves and leave the planning for another day. They would discuss it the next day, now was about results and what they had achieved. One thing they agreed was that something needed to be stepped up with the Sun. They were invincible, and it was time the group brought them back down to earth. Nobody had ever even challenged them.

This was now time for actual change. It was again time for the people to stand up to journalists who have had the freedom to destroy people's lives without punishment, and all to sell some newspapers.

Chapter 14

Anew day and the sun was shining across Castle Drum. After leaving The Fox Bar around eight the previous evening, there had been a few sore heads in most of the group. They had a great day and cheered Andy up. They chatted about everything from cars, football, and politics, which continued for a while. Most of them agreed that the country was a political mess, with only the conservative party as a genuine option, and even that didn't excite them much.

'I really feel for Andy,' said Chelsea as she went back into the bedroom with a coffee for Gary.

'Me too, honey.'

'You said we would discuss these plans today; do you really feel up for it?'

'Fuck yeah! A shower and chill out for a few hours, and we'll meet up with them later. We can't let this sit too long, especially for Andy's mental health. He has been obsessed with this, and he needs our help. We just can't let the lad down.'

Gary pulled himself out of bed and headed to the shower with coffee in hand.

'Donna has just texted me. She's asking if we want to go to the cinema tonight.' Chelsea told Gary.

'I'm up for that, but rule out any fucking chick flick.' Chelsea knew he wasn't serious.

Steven wore sunglasses for Ben's walk. He arrived back feeling terrible and asked himself why hadn't come home earlier the night before. It was becoming more common for him to stay out later than usual and suffer the consequences the next day. Although he knew he was lying to himself when he promised not to do it again, it would always happen. He would convince himself that he was still young and should be having a good time until the next time. Something most people did and justified it as just human nature.

'Hey, princess,' Steven called out as he released Ben from his leash at the front door.

'Hi, darling. Was it worth it?' Donna saw the self-pity on Steven's face.

'I'm never doing that again.' Steven threw himself onto the couch and picked up the remote control for the TV.

'We need to do it again tonight. Well, maybe not as many, but I have asked Chelsea and Gary if they would like to go to the cinema tonight, so a few pre-movie drinks will make you feel better,' said Donna as she lay on top of Steven on the couch.

They began kissing and, within minutes, had stripped their clothes. Hangover sex was great. They both loved it.

Donna sat on top of him and was riding him like there was no tomorrow. Steven was trying to enjoy the moment, but Ben wanted attention, and he had to push him away on a couple of occasions before yelling at him to get to bed.

They stood up; Steven pushed her against the wall with her breasts pressed against it; he took her from behind. Thrusting inside her and pulling the back of her hair, Donna was moaning in delight. They were both ecstatic and made passionate love for the next fifteen minutes. Sweating, they fell back to the couch and cuddled in silence for a few minutes.

'That was fucking awesome sex.' Donna kissed him a few times in quick succession.

'It was indeed, my princess. I love you so much.'

'I love you too, but it's time for a shower and to get ready to do something rather than sit around all day. The weather is beautiful,' she said as they proceeded to the shower for round two of sex before getting dressed and heading for the door and a walk into Castle Drum shops.

Brad didn't make it home. He decided he would go home with Andy for another couple of beers, which wasn't the best idea. Andy sneaked off to bed less than ten minutes after opening them both a beer.

'How are you feeling, mate?' Brad asked Andy as he appeared from the bedroom and opened the living room curtains.

'Not sure if I'm still drunk or dead.' Andy put the kettle on.

'It was a great night, though. I really enjoyed it. I can't wait to hit these bastards and get really involved,' said Brad.

'Coffee?' Andy shouted.

Brad nodded.

'Yes, I had a great night. It's good that everyone can help, and I don't have it all on my own shoulders now. I hope we don't leave it too long.' Andy said.

'Chelsea has just messaged me. The four of them are going to the cinema tonight and asking if I'm up for it too?' Brad asked.

'The fucking cinema, with two couples?' Andy laughed as he picked up his phone. 'I got the same message. The six of us are better than two couples, I suppose.'

All agreed to meet in the Carlton Bar, only a four-minute walk from the cinema. The movie was an action movie. A good cop, bad cop chasing drug dealers in the US. Surveillance. Apt for them!

It had been a while since any of them had visited the Carlton Bar. Years, not months, but nothing had really changed. It was an old-fashioned bar, like going back in time. A bar that relied on regulars rather than tourists. People knew what to expect, and there weren't modern furnishings. The chandeliers were plastic, looked like no one had cleaned them before or after the no-smoking ban that came into place on first July, two thousand and seven. Dull yellow lighting was the theme, which matched the outdated brown tables and chairs, some of which had people's names scratched on them with keys or small knives. One name read Davy 2000, which gave them a clue on how management ran the place. All that didn't matter. They didn't intend to stay long.

There was time enough for a few beers and ciders before the cinema. Steven joked he had just walked from 1983 to

2020 in four minutes. They had only opened the cinema for around nine months; it was modern but pricey. They spent around fifty-five pounds on drinks and sweets, with the women spending the most on pick and mix.

'We should have brought our own,' said Steven.

'It's not allowed,' Donna reminded him.

'That's a myth. There is nothing stopping anyone from bringing sweets, drinks, or food here. It's just not the thing to do unless you're coming pretty often. The expensive food keeps the price of the tickets down. I worked in a cinema in my younger days.' Brad pointed out.

'Next time, it's the supermarket for multipacks,' Steven suggested as they found screen number seven on the second floor.

They took their seats, completely in awe of the sound system. It was phenomenal. The sound was coming at them from every direction. The screen was the biggest any of them had ever seen. They had undoubtedly upgraded the cinema experience since any of them last attended. Although they all disapproved of the twenty-two minutes of adverts and trailers, such was life.

The movie started. There were some funny parts between the two cops that had the audience in fits of laughter. One was severe, and the other a bit of a loose cannon. A partnership made in hell for the more sensible cop. Both cops looked out for an essential witness in their drugs case, but the witness had been challenging to track down. They had a tip-off he the bowling alley somewhere in California, so they went undercover in the car park. The witness arrived back at his car and the cops pulled up, blocking him in.

They both jumped out of the car. The good cop attends to the car's driver's side and prevents the driver from getting out. He shows identification and instructs the driver to turn off the engine. He complies. The funny, loose cannon of a cop appears at the front of the car with a huge plastic toy Nerf water gun he pulled from the boot of his car. This has the audience in fits of laughter again. This crazy cop is threatening the driver with a fully loaded water gun. The witness had agreed that he would show up on the court date, but the crazy cop explained that it was not good enough and that he had been too difficult to find. They had made a deal, and the witness had not kept his own end of the agreement.

'Do you want to go back to prison? We made a deal!' shouted the crazy cop in his American accent. 'You're too hard to find, motherfucker. It will be easier to get you if you don't have a car. I'm going to shoot your fucking tyres out.'

The cop went round the tyres and made shooting noises like a kid would do in the playground. He fired several shots at each tyre, doing no more damage than getting them soaking wet.

'I'll clean your windows; maybe you'll see things more clearly.'

The witness agreed and updated the good cop with his latest address and telephone number and the reasons he never showed up at the previous court date; a death in the family. He promised he would appear next time. The good cop accepted this and made his way back to the patrol car.

'You're going nowhere, motherfucker!' The crazy cop pulled out a lighter and threw it at the driver's side wheel. It burst into flames as he walked back to his car. The Nerf gun had been full of petrol; within seconds, the shots fired at the ground spread. All four wheels were alight.

Steven leaned forward to see past Donna and looked at the rest of the group. Their eyes were like rabbits in headlights for a few seconds, all understanding what had just happened. As previously discussed, there was no need for them to use a petrol can. They would all use kids' toys. All six of them burst out laughing with the rest of the audience, but they were laughing at something else only the six of them understood. The movie gave them a plan.

'I don't believe that just happened,' Gary said as they made their way out of the cinema.

'Unbelievable.' Chelsea and Donna laughed simultaneously.

'It's meant to be. It's a sign.' Gary laughed.

'Who's for another few drinks?' Andy was excited.

They'd had enough of the Carlton Bar for the next five years and moved back to The Fox Bar for drinks but on the condition only a few. Two taxis drew up for their ten-minute journey across town.

Gary ordered a round of drinks as the others took the same seats they had the night before. They discussed the previous night's antics and laughed at their group attempt at karaoke shortly before they left. They discussed how much they murdered Frank Sinatra's My Way, to the amusement of the customers and bar staff.

'I got it,' said Gary as he arrived at the table clenching pints of cider.

'We'll chip in for the round, mate. Don't worry yourself,' quipped Steven.

'No, not that, you idiot! We dress as clowns with Nerf guns. Who's going to expect that? Think about it.' Gary laughed. 'I'm a fucking genius.'

Going for a pleasant night out had become a planning evening over a couple of drinks. As they previously discussed, the Anonymous masks were no longer an option. They were becoming too far-leftists, and they wished to disassociate any connection. If they were to get caught, anything Anonymous carried out would be pinned on them, and they were now fighting different battles. After discussing routes, who was doing what, who would speak, what message to leave the target, and where it would take place, they were moving at pace, to the delight of Andy.

It would take place after Christine McDonald took the children to school. Five minutes past nine precisely, on the corner of Bankglen Avenue and Chesters Road. They would walk out in front of the car, dressed as clowns and having fun with the guns, but not squirting each other. It would draw attention, but it wouldn't strike fear into anyone. Clowns being clowns. Donna and Chelsea would take the lead in dancing, as none of the guys volunteered. The four lads would gather around the car and start spraying the wheels. Then the women would then hold up a sign in front of the vehicle before it was up in flames. They hoped Christine would get out of the car then.

'Two days, let's do it then,' everyone nodded in agreement with Gary.

'I have all I need at home; I got the same for Brad, so we can meet you all there. I will buy the guns at two different shops on the way home,' Andy offered.

After listing the materials they needed and who was buying what, they went home. Most of them planned a day of doing absolutely fuck all but chilling at home. Online catch-up with the underground news and other events carried out by different groups across Europe, movies, or sleeping most of the day appealed to Chelsea and Donna.

Everything was in place. Andy wanted to tell them the exact reason they were being targeted, but all that would do was narrow down the police search to a family member. Andy trusted the group, and they trusted him. He wanted to see the fear on her face. He wanted her to run away to Daddy and tell him what had happened. His day was about to become a reality, and it was time the Sun wasn't shining.

Chapter 15

Andy didn't sleep much. He was on edge, overthinking how he was going to go through with his plan. He had all the materials required and Brad was to arrive in the next hour at his flat. Then they would drive to the location.

Andy had let himself go for weeks. Sadly, he had neglected himself and his flat. There was rubbish lying on the floor next to the full bin bags. It was as though he didn't care anymore. The event was the only thing on his mind, and he convinced himself that once this was over, he would give himself a shake and find his lost energy.

As usual, Brad arrived right on time and knocked on the door with his fist rather than using the letterbox or doorbell. It was just the way he was, trying to terrify people with his police officer knock.

'Slight change of plan, mate,' Andy told Brad.

'What do you mean?'

'I need to go somewhere first, but wearing the clown suit and with the guns. It won't take too long; we can leave fifteen minutes early.'

Brad and Andy jumped in the car and headed off.

'Take the next right here, Brad. Next left and continue to the end of the road.'

'Where are we going? We are heading off the planned route, mate.' Brad sounded concerned.

'We're nearly there; pull in next to the traffic lights.' Andy pointed to a space behind a Post Office van.

'OK, I'm getting out here. You head down that street there,' said Andy, indicating a narrower, quieter, one-way street. 'I'll be there in a few minutes.'

Andy was calm, speaking in a low voice.

'Andy, what the fuck is going on? We'll be late!'

Andy pulled on his clown mask and opened the passenger door.

'Just go. Wait down there.'

He walked to the other side of the road and started dancing, waving the gun around in the air. The area was tranquil with few people around and almost no cars. It wasn't exactly in the centre of town.

Andy was out of the car minutes when he saw a black Mercedes Benz GLA approaching him. It was getting close. Andy danced along the middle of the road and almost stood in the car's path. He looked like a raving lunatic dressed in a clown outfit waving a toy gun about his head. The Mercedes belonged to Raymond Park-Smith and, as expected, the car slowed down enough to allow Andy to jump in front of it. Raymond carried out an emergency stop. As soon as the car was stationary, Andy slowly danced around the car while spraying petrol over the vehicle. Raymond couldn't smell the petrol from inside the car. He thought it was water. The first thing he did was to put his windscreen wipers on. Andy never uttered a word. The gun was almost half empty, and there was no way he could move from the front of the car because Raymond would drive off.

'You motherfucker, Raymond Park-Smith! You have blood on your hands.'

Raymond put the car in reverse. This wasn't a clown dancing in the street; this was a set-up.

Andy pulled a lighter from his pocket and scratched it against the car's front. There was a vast blue flash as all the petrol ignited.

'Editor of a scum newspaper. We, the people, won't take any more of your lies. You fucking horrible bastard! You are a murderer!'

Raymond reversed as fast as he could in his now burning Mercedes.

Once the flames engulfed the car's front, Andy noticed his gloves were on fire. He threw the toy gun on the ground and pulled the gloves off. The toy gun was now in flames in the middle of the road. Andy made a run for it back to the car to join Brad.

'Where the fuck are Brad and Andy?' Gary asked.

'I know. It's strange because it's really his gig.' Donna sounded concerned.

'It's almost time,' Chelsea reminded them.

'We'll need to carry this out alone. We'll take two tyres each. Steven, on the same side, back and front. Girls, nothing has changed for you two. OK?'

It was now three minutes to nine. Eight minutes before Christine should arrive and six minutes before they needed to walk the short distance to the crossroads where the event would take place. They dressed with only the masks left. It was time to go. Once out of the car, they danced around in case anyone was watching from nearby. They didn't want to look suspicious. Clowns don't look half as suspect as folk wearing black clothing with balaclavas.

They were in position when they saw a car coming towards them. It was Christine's BMW. They danced on the road, drawing her to a complete stop. Donna and Chelsea stood in front of the car while Gary walked round to the driver's door.

'Step out of the car!'

Gary pointed a huge toy Nerf gun at the driver's window. Christine laughed.

'I said, "Step out of the car," Christine,' Gary repeated.

In a split second, the look on her face went from happiness to fear. Gary opened the driver's door.

'Good morning, Christine, can you please get out of the car.? We loaded these guns with petrol, and we're going to burn your car right now. We don't want you to get hurt.'

Christine was now in shock. She grabbed her bag and stepped out of the car.

'Open fire!' Steven shouted to Gary as they sprayed the car with petrol.

'Come over here, Christine,' Chelsea ordered. 'We will explain who we are. We are from a group called The People For The People. Some describe us as vigilantes, but we make sure nobody gets hurt, so we prefer Superhero Clowns. Are you listening to me?'

'Yes, yes.'

'Your father has been a very naughty boy as editor of the Scum newspaper. We've had enough of his lies and bullying of victims. This is your father's fault. We know he doesn't give a fuck about anything or anyone, but this is a warning to him, not you. We really are sorry for the inconvenience.' Donna and Chelsea sniggered.

'Please inform your father that he is putting you, himself, and your two brothers in danger. We know your brothers no longer live in the UK, but we know where to find them. Our agenda is to change the unaccountable UK Scum media that prints lies daily. We are sick of reading what our media sources tell us with no proof. Fake news is not just an online thing. Newspapers in this county need to report authentic stories. Do you know how many children go missing in the UK each year? How many never return?' Donna was ranting.

'Time's up. Let's go!' Gary shouted as Steven lit a match and threw it towards the car.

Christine stood silently with her hand over her mouth.

'Now you make sure the first person you call when we leave is your dad, and then the fire brigade. Do you understand?' Chelsea said.

'Moving out, now!' Gary shouted.

They ran towards their parked car around the corner and out of Christine's view. They took off their masks; only Gary driving was visible to anyone looking in the car, as the others ducked down in their seats. Christine's car was ablaze. A few locals came out to assist her, so she wasn't alone anymore. The group followed the plan and headed back to Gary's flat.

What was about to be news was that Andy had carried out the same stunt on Christine's father's car minutes earlier. He hadn't stopped quickly enough and had still been in the blazing car when they last saw him.

They had gone straight to Andy's house, stripped off the costumes, and changed back into their regular clothes. It amused Andy when Brad suggested he keep the outfit on for the rest of the week. Brad thought he was losing the plot.

It was now nine-fifteen. Gary sent Andy a text. *Meet at mine in twenty minutes.'*

Andy acknowledged with a wink and a thumbs up, but was more nervous than before, as he wasn't sure how the rest of them would react to his solo adventure.

'Where the fuck were you?' Gary stared at Andy as he walked through Gary's front door.

'What's happened to your hand?' Chelsea grabbed Andy's arm and saw a sizeable burn on the back of his right hand was.

'Look, I'm sorry. It was an impulsive move, and Brad knew nothing about it.'

'I only knew what was going on when it happened; I thought we were taking a quick detour before meeting up with you guys.'

'What the fuck are you talking about?' Gary stared at them both.

Andy took a seat and told them the details of what happened and how he burned his hand. Gary was furious for a few minutes, but seemed to see the bigger picture.

'We've pulled off a double stunt. This is not what we planned, but it can benefit us. So, you pulled this off alone? You fucking mental bastard! Do you wish for a prison sentence? What if—'

'If fuck all Gary. Nothing happened; it's done. I lay in bed all last night. Maybe I had three hours of sleep, possibly two. Something told me I was targeting the wrong person, and it wouldn't have had as much impact as he didn't give a fuck about anyone, including his own daughter.' Andy was now in a state.

'Let's look at that,' said Donna, taking Andy into the kitchen and running his hand under cold water. 'You need to keep it under there for around thirty minutes.'

'OK, thanks, but if I'm going to be here thirty minutes, I need a beer for the other hand!' Andy joked, then shouted. 'Any beers in the fridge, Gary?'

'Top shelf, you fucker!'

Once they were in the kitchen, they shared how the morning's events had gone. They got two birds with one stone.

A double warning to the smug bastard, Raymond Park-Smith. Surely, he needed to take caution now that he and his family had been involved in an incident. Anyone in their right mind would consider that things could be a lot worse next time.

'Don't you ever do anything like that again! If you want to be part of this, we need discipline. What if we had abandoned the match because you never turned up? There are so many possibilities that could have come from this. Who was looking out for you while you were going off on one? What if a member of the public came to assist the prick? You would have been safer with more of us around. Anyway, it's done now, so tell me, how did it feel?' He put an arm round Brad. 'How's the hand?'

'I think it looks a lot worse than it actually is.'

'So, are you happy with how things have gone, Gary? You're not going to continue stalking the Sun, are you? There's not much we can hope for regarding feedback for this one; I mean, he's hardly going to report this in his own paper.'

Steven opened the fridge and grabbed a beer.

'Anyone else?' he offered.

At that, his phone received a WhatsApp message which read: *Phone me a.s.a.p.*

Steven thought to himself, 'What this fuck does he want?'

Just at that moment, a video appeared of a clown on the road. *Has this anything to do with you? Lol. It's at your neck of the woods.* Some laughing emojis followed this. Steven opened the video to see footage of Andy dressed as a clown and shouting abuse at a Mercedes car.

'What the fuck! That didn't take long. It's less than a fucking hour.' Steven started the video from the beginning for the others.

'This is brilliant,' Gary said. 'Where did that come from?'

'I'm not sure, but it looks like someone has filmed it from the new flats on Grange Road. I just got it from one lad online. He knew it was in my area.'

'Deny all knowledge right away. Throw him off the scent.'

Steven called and told his mate, Asteroid, saying he knew nothing about it.

'The poor bastard making his way to work and having to put up with some crazy clown. What's the world coming to, eh?' Steven made a face.

'Poor bastard. According to Twitter, that's Raymond Park-Smith's car,' Asteroid informed him.

'Am I supposed to know him? Keeping up with the latest celebrities is not my thing,' Steven said jovially.

'He's the editor-in-chief at the Sun, you clown,' said Asteroid. 'No pun intended.'

'Fuck off! The cunt deserves it then. I'm all for clowns these days.'

Steven ended the call with the promise to catch up one day. He made out that he'd been busy with work and a new relationship and didn't have the time these days to hang around forums all day. He knew that meeting would never happen, though.

'I have just been told it's on Twitter, and it was the editor of the Sun's car!' Steven smiled as the rest pulled out their phones. People had only posted it only a few times, but it was still early.

'Everyone get sharing and retweeting,' said Gary.

The video didn't do as well as they had hoped, but the abuse the Sun received was priceless. People started tagging the Sun, and the group noticed a few unexpected hashtags. #Thepeopleforthepeople, #SunScum and #PeoplePower. They needed to ramp things up, and Twitter was the way to go.

'Take this list of hashtags, log in to Twitter and get this trending.' Gary passed an old notepad to Steven.

'What's this?'

'My eighty-eight Twitter accounts, all with at least five thousand followers.' He winked. 'Eighty-eight is a lucky number for the Chinese and me, so I kept that number.'

'Shall we hook in for help?' Steven suggested.

'I'm already on it, mate.'

Gary approached his desktop computer running on Linux operating system. They sat next to each other at the desk and expected the numbers to increase. It was approaching lunchtime. Many people at work would be on Twitter, whether in Starbucks or sitting on the toilet.

Gary was logging in and running many bits of software while Steven sat in awe of his skills. Steven knew all about the hacking and wished he could do it, but got no further than reading a few articles and books. He was interested in what was happening before his eyes. Gary talked them through making everything secure before going back to the forum.

Brad hung over the back of Gary's black leather office chair.

'Eighteen hundred and seventy-three messages! Fucking hell, mate. You're a popular one on here.'

'He doesn't know, does he?' Steven looked at Gary.

'Know what?' Brad looked between Gary and the things he was doing on screen. Several boxes opened and flashed, requesting passwords. It differed from what Brad understood a computer was. When someone mentioned computers to Brad, he always thought of Windows Vista.

'Know what?' Brad repeated.

'Can I tell him and save you from blowing your own trumpet?'

Gary just nodded. He was busy doing what he knew. Nobody else had a clue.

'You're in the company of one of the world's most famous hackers. A celebrity on the underground internet.'

'What, like these guys who hack companies? Fuck off! You're taking the piss. OK, tell me who you have hacked before.' Brad suggested.

'Vodafone, AOL, Yahoo, Nintendo, UK Revenue and Customs, to name but a few,' Gary admitted, while still concentrating on what was happening online with the group.

'Are you that justice guy I heard about that nobody has ever traced and is still on the run?' Brad laughed out loud. He didn't have a clue how relevant his comment was.

Brad had only ever heard of this person through his younger brother and friends. They had regarded him as a hero a few years back and would spend a couple of hours chatting about his conquests.

'Do you mean Midnight Justice?'

'That's the one. My brother thinks he's a fucking legend.'

Gary spun around in the leather chair and looked Brad directly in the eyes.

'You need to keep this between us if I tell you my name. Promise?' Gary sounded serious.

'I promise!'

'Online, I have tens of thousands of followers, and my name on there is—' Gary looked at Steven before shouting, 'Fred Flintstone!' They burst out laughing.

'What does your brother do online if he knows famous hackers?' Gary was curious.

'You're asking the wrong person, mate. I only hear the conversations between him and his mates either over at his place or down the pub. I don't have a clue,' replied Brad.

'The one you mentioned, Midnight, his name is Midnight Justice. I know him. Is that the one your brother speaks about?'

'That's him. I remember my brother and his mate having a debate about if Midnight was male or female.' Brad's comments made it difficult for the others to control their laughter.

'I can't keep a straight face anymore!' Chelsea yelled, which made everyone else laugh except for a lost Brad, who still hadn't caught on.

'Brad. It's about time.' Gary put his hand out.

'I'm Midnight Justice,' Gary admitted as he grabbed Brad's hand, shook it and turned back to the screen.

Steven looked at Brad with a smile and nodded to back up what Gary had just said. Brad sat back on the couch in disbelief. Midnight Justice's stories came flooding back from times in his brother's garden. With his mates, he had spoken about hackers the way people talked about football in the UK. Midnight Justice was a celebrity to his younger brother.

'Have you done?' Brad asked, but Gary interrupted.

'I'll answer all your questions in around nine minutes. I'm at work here, and this is very important. You will all see the results soon,' Gary continued to send and receive messages. To the others, the information on the screen might as well be in Chinese. Nobody understood a thing.

'Can someone check the Sun's website, please?' Gary watched them type on their phones.

'It's down,' Donna reported.

'Try again now,' said Gary.

'Oh, my fucking God!' was the simultaneous response from Donna and Chelsea.

'This is gold. Outfuckingstanding,' said Steven.

Andy looked over Chelsea's shoulder at her phone. His hand was now wrapped in a clean bandage.

'This is incredible. Did you just do that, mate?' asked Andy.

In the hour that passed, Gary had played his part and made the Sun homepage into a massive picture of a clown. With help from others somewhere around the world, when people clicked on the clown's red nose, the video of Andy attacking Raymond's car would also play the soundtrack of Power to the People by John Lennon. It was genius. The message at the bottom of the screen was just perfect.

It's time for the UK mainstream media to wake up and report the truth. We are a group called The People For The People and have had enough of your lies, misinformation, irrelevant news, scare stories, celebrity bullshit, cover-ups, and much more. It's time to get back to basics. The People For The People will be watching. We know more about you than you know about us.

Be careful; you could be next.

Lots of Peace and Love X

TPFTP.

Within ten minutes, the Sun was trending on Twitter across the UK. The tweets were going so fast it was impossible to read them all. They counted around seventy-nine tweets per minute.

Donna looked at Andy; he was emotional but held back the tears.

'This was for you, kid,' Andy said as he pointed to the sky.

'Aw, Andy, that's so sweet.' Donna gave him a hug.

'Midnight Justice just pulled off a masterstroke right in front of my eyes,' said a shocked Brad.

'Who's for celebrating?' asked Steven.

Everyone shouted their individual positive responses so that nobody could make anything out.

'Who's for champagne? I'm going to the shops,' said Steven as he raised his now empty cider can, squashed it and threw it directly into the open bin on the other side of the room.

'I'll come with you,' Brad said, as they left to pick up more alcohol and snacks.

It was just as well Brad volunteered to go with Steven, as he would never have managed on his own. They were in and out of the supermarket and purchased three bottles of Moet & Chandon, and a twenty-four crate of Magner's cider, as well as two bags full of snacks. Steven knew he would need to eat with drinking, especially at that time of day.

'Do you think Gary would meet my brother?' Brad asked as they neared the entrance to Gary's place.

'All you can do is ask, mate. What does your brother do for a living?'

'He does what Gary does, just not anything as big. He's a hacktivist and has the same political opinions as us. It might be useful. I know he would be willing. One hundred percent.'

He was desperate for his brother to meet Midnight Justice.

Back at the flat, they heard a countdown from the others.

'Five, four, three, two, one!' followed by an enormous cheer.

'You won't believe this,' Chelsea said. 'One hundred thousand retweets in less than an hour. It's on fire!'

The group stayed at Gary's, drinking champagne and cider as they followed the UK's most discussed topic. Other UK newspapers started reporting it, and rival newspapers jumped on it and destroyed the Sun with humour. Memes were everywhere. They had created something yet again, but all they gave the credit to Andy this time.

'This is all yours, mate.' Gary looked at Andy, who was a little drunk.

'If you didn't go rogue, then we would have needed to wait on some kind of sign that they changed their ways, but now it's everywhere. They have to take note, not just them, all of them.' Gary saw a satisfied, smiling Andy.

Brad was as drunk as the rest of them. He stumbled, almost crashing into the table in the middle of the living area.

'Gary, I want you to meet my brother; you'll make his fucking day,' slurred Brad. 'Honestly, he's a top lad. Just like the rest of us, he's amazing with computers. It's what he does for a living. Not sure if he's at your level, as I don't know much about them. In fact, I could say I could write my knowledge of computers on the back of a stamp with a crayon.' He laughed.

'What does your brother do?' Gary saw the others were listening.

'I'm not sure exactly, something to do with computer-related security systems for the BBC. Not directly; he's a contractor. He earns a decent wage.'

The group looked at each other. There was silence for the first time since early that morning.

'Did you just say the BBC?' Gary gulped.

Chapter 16

The Sun released a statement. It was nothing worth shouting about. They ranted about freedom of the press and how they wouldn't be intimidated by attacks like TPFTP; even going as low as pointing out that attacking cars would only drive up the average public members' insurance premiums. Somehow, they thought they were the victims after everything they had reported against innocent people over the years. They didn't even bother to mention that Christine's car was also attacked. Absolute Scum.

The group still saw it as a victory and enjoyed their celebrations into the night, with headaches the following day. They felt like a unit, genuine close friends, fighting for the same cause. They were part of something none of them had ever dreamed of. Everyone was talking about the Sun. It was all over social media for a couple of days, and when they released their statement, it refuelled the fire. Still, only six people knew who was responsible.

Gary was drunk at the flat that night and asked Brad to send him a message as a reminder. He didn't want to forget Brad's brother. Gary looked at his phone. *Meet Kevin* was all it said in the last text from Brad. He decided he would meet with him that day after work.

'Brad, mate! How are you feeling?' Gary spoke into the office phone.

'I don't know why I do it, mate. The hangovers are unreal. I'm OK, but not one hundred percent yet.'

'Have you told your brother Kevin anything about me yet?'

'No, to be honest, I haven't seen him.'

'Can you give him a phone and see if he fancies meeting up later? Maybe around six-thirty? Fox Bar? We need to talk.'

Gary heard Brad's voice change as he agreed.

'But don't tell him who I am. I will tell him tonight. See you then, mate.'

Gary put the phone down and packed his bag. Five hours in the office was enough for the day as he headed out to grab some food before meeting the brothers.

'You must be Kevin,' Gary gave both of them a firm handshake as they stood at the front door of the pub.

'How are you doing, lad, OK?' Kevin grinned at Gary. 'Brad told me you are handy with computers, is that right?'

'Yeah, I have done a thing or two with them in my spare time.'

Brad turned away to hide what could have been laughter but controlled himself.

At The Fox Bar, they ordered drinks. Kevin preferred a Captain Morgan and Coke Zero, rather than a cider.

'Hard day at the office?' Kevin opened up the conversation.

'Not really, just Groundhog Day. A few security checks and stayed around longer than I should have just to justify my job,' said Gary. 'I hear you're a bit of a hacktivist.'

'I try to do my bit for society. I fucking hate the US pharmaceutical companies. What they get away with is incredible. Did you know an inhaler for asthma in the US can be one hundred and twenty dollars, but it can cost as little as thirty-five cents in Cuba! It's criminal.'

'Do you remember there was an incident with the owner of Medicod not so long ago?' Gary asked Kevin.

'Yes, I do. It was phenomenal. That bastard Colin Oscar-Douglas deserved everything that came his way. A horrible bastard of a man.'

'Yes, I agree. Can I trust this guy?' Gary nodded toward Brad.

'He's my brother; of course you can. Are you going to spill the beans and let him join us?'

He winked at a clueless Kevin, who was wondering what the fuck was going on, looking backwards and forwards at them both as if he was watching tennis.

'That Medicod incident. That was me,' admitted Gary.

'Fuck off! Seriously?'

'One hundred percent, bro. Me too.' Brad sported a huge grin.

'Is this some kind of fucking wind up?'

'Do you remember that time you and a couple of your mates were having a debate about a hacktivist? You were all discussing if the person was a man or a woman?' Brad reminded him.

'Yes, I remember. Midnight Justice? We discussed the man or woman issue.'

'Kevin, meet Midnight Justice.'

Kevin's eyes looked like he had just seen a million-pound lottery ticket with his name on it and almost choked on his rum. He quickly removed the glass from his mouth and wiped some spillage from his chin.

'Hold on a fucking minute here. My brother is involved in all this, and you're one of the most well-known hackers worldwide, and here we are sitting in The Fucking Fox Bar? Do you two think I'm fucking stupid?'

'You're here because I told Gary about you when we were celebrating our last mission. What you do and where you work.'

'And that mission was?' Kevin's curiosity got the better of him.

Gary took out his phone and handed it to Kevin. It had screenshots of the Sun homepage, and he then showed him the video that was uploaded. Kevin sat thinking for a few minutes with a massive grin on his face.

'That Sun stunt was fucking amazing. It went viral for a few days. It was superb!'

'Yes, we enjoyed it,' said Brad.

'Stop right there. Are you two taking credit for this too? Who the fuck is my brother? I don't even know you these days.' Kevin placed his hand on his brother's shoulder. 'This is all too fucking much to take in. Fuck me dead.'

He leaned back in his seat.

'We want you to join us, and then we will tell you everything that we have done to date. Your skills and experience can advise us. We are planning the BBC next. Don't worry; nobody will get hurt. It's about time these paedophile sheltering bastards were exposed and defunded,' said Gary. 'Think about it.'

'If this is genuine, what do you expect from me?' Kevin asked.

Over a few drinks, they told him about the groups Gary used to be part of and their present group, explaining the difference and why they no longer wish to be associated with Anonymous. They discussed what would be necessary to carry out the plans they had for the BBC. Kevin gave them significant input. He wanted to be involved.

After ten minutes, he acknowledged Midnight Justice, told Gary it was great to meet him and gave him another firm handshake. They also discussed the fact that they had previously chatted in the underground forums a couple of times, but Gary's memory failed him because he had spoken to hundreds, if not thousands, of people over the years.

Kevin was very enthusiastic. He couldn't stay still in the seat, so paced up and down. He felt like he was sitting with a celebrity because Gary was precisely that in his world. His mates would be envious of him that night.

'You can't tell anyone, lad. These random things happen safely because only we on the ground and a few online know what's going on. Not even your friends can know. Look how well Brad kept this from you,' said Gary.

'I totally understand. Not a problem. I won't tell a soul.'

'Welcome to The People For The People Brother,' said Brad.

Brad was delighted that Kevin agreed with everything the group stood for. Everyone agreed. Kevin was an easy-going lad and very intelligent. He would fit into the group because he got along with everyone. He lived alone and wasn't much of a party animal, given that he was twenty-seven. He preferred to drink at home or at a friend's house. He always said there are too many arseholes in pubs, and after nine in any city, things can become dangerous and unpredictable. It just wasn't his scene. He was around six foot and had blonde hair. Not long down his back, more like what Boris Johnson's hair would be like if he brushed it.

The three of them sat and talked, without more drinks, for the next hour. They threw ideas at each other and suggested what they could do at the BBC. Kevin ruled out some adventurous things, but agreed that more than a few of their ideas were possible with his help. They all agreed and listed what would be their agenda.

- The fight against corruption around the world.
- Stricter punishment for MPs breaking their own rules.
- An investigation into conflict of interest with MPs and pharmaceutical companies, also the NHS private contracts.
- Pushing MPs further for genuine investigations into corruption.
- The abolition of the UK TV licence.
- The BBC cover-up of paedophilia.
- Genuine effort in tackling homelessness and people with disabilities, child poverty and missing children.
- More funding and assistance for our own ex-forces.

- An investigation into the value of funding overseas and more transparency.

- More stock market regulation to protect retail investors and not just giant corporations.

If they were going to pull this off, they needed to include as many issues as possible to gain public support in what could become a global audience.

Kevin had access to so many things. Security cameras, access points, the BBC websites, employee databases, including contractors like himself, the ability to give clearance, he could even copy some security passes. However, most of this would be hacking, as they had limited his access to the security of the internal IT systems.

Kevin knew others in the BBC security teams, and many hated the BBC.

'What about getting some others on board?'

'Like who?' asked Gary.

'Many of the security are great guys. They are just like us but are looked down on by many BBC management. Celebrities are the fucking worst, though. Management is all snobby upper-class twats who think these security lads are working class scum. I know a few who wouldn't stand in your way to enter the building for the weekly take-home pay that they receive. It's just something to think about. I won't say a thing without your approval; Midnight... I mean Gary.'

'You could be onto something, lad,' replied Gary.

'How many security lads do we need to get by to be where exactly where we need to be?' Brad asked Kevin.

'You have the main reception, and then you are in the building. Entry is by security pass, and everything else depends on what level of pass you have. If you had A1 passes, you could basically open every door in the place. Unlimited access. But there are many security lads on various floors, which is where the security rota will come in handy. I can find out who is on what floor. They rarely change. Michael, for example, has been on the fourth floor for nearly two years.' Kevin explained to Gary.

'And can we get A1 passes?'

'Of course we can; I can hack into one director's account and make as many as I want. It will then look like he has issued them personally. The only tough part would be to pick up the cards and the reader that puts the details on them.'

'What about storing the details on a memory stick, and I get the equipment to put it on the cards at home? I know someone who has one,' said Gary.

'Yes, that's not a problem. We will be sorted if you can get the reader, but it would make sense to have a trial run first just to make sure.' Kevin suggested.

Kevin couldn't hide his excitement at what could happen.

'To be honest, guys, if this is a success, I couldn't really give a fuck if I lost my job. It would be all worth it.'

They agreed that what they were about to pull off would be more significant than any hack they had carried out to date and would have global headlines. The enthusiasm meant they would have one for the road.

Chapter 17

Steven woke up beside Donna. It was eleven-thirty. More than a few hours after their usual body clock alarm, but that was down to watching movies in bed till around four in the morning. Even Ben didn't wake them for his regular walk, as he sensed the heavy rain outside.

The minute Steven got out of bed, he thought of coffee, grabbed his phone and switched it on. He walked to the living room, leaving Donna in bed, stretching and talking to Ben.

'I have seven missed calls and four messages from Gary,' he shouted to Donna.

'Anything important?' she asked as she got out from under the warm, cosy duvet into the cooler air of the bedroom.

She donned her dressing gown.

'He says the plan is in his head. We are going global. Be prepared.'

'You do know that he always exaggerates things, right?'

'The last message is about dinner. Our place or his tonight?' Steven repeated the message.

'I'll cook. Who's coming round?' asked Donna.

'Not sure. I'll reply later. What shall we do today, honey?'

Gary and Chelsea were out of their flat early. With no hangover, he was buzzing with adrenaline. Things happened for a reason, and meeting Kevin was a sign that this next stunt had to be done. When he got back from The Fox Bar the previous night, he told Chelsea the plans.

'I really want to be a big part of this,' Chelsea said as they drove into the town centre.

'What do you mean?' asked Gary

'I want to be with you and the others. I'm not going to be sitting in the car waiting. If we need a getaway driver, get someone else.'

'I can imagine it now. The four of us will take centre stage. I have dreamed of this for a very long time. You will be beside me, sweetheart. Don't worry.' Gary reassured her.

'If we do this with planning to the finest detail, nothing can go wrong.'

'That's why I have chosen a date two weeks away. We can't do this with only the group. We need help from others. I know it's not the way we wanted to do things, but we need to get back on the forums for something on this scale. We need as many people as possible in on this.'

They approached the indoor shopping centre car park to begin some retail therapy.

'I have just messaged Chelsea. She and Gary are in town. Shall we meet them?' Donna suggested.

'Yes, I'm hungry and can't be bothered cooking. Will they still be there in forty minutes?'

In thirty minutes, Steven and Donna showered, did the little housework, and took Ben for a walk. Steven knew nothing about Gary's plans, but knew he would come up with something worthwhile.

Steven ordered a taxi for the short distance. Time was getting on and almost at the agreed meeting time. He planned to have a full English breakfast and mug of tea at the Oasis Cafe. The food at Oasis was always fantastic. He had been a frequent visitor until he cut down on the morning fry ups.

'Good morning, you ugly bastard and Donna,' Gary greeted them.

'Good morning Chelsea, what the fuck do you see in him?' asked Steven.

Chelsea and Donna gave each other a hug and sat down at a table. The typical cafe table with the red and white striped table cloth, loaded with ketchup bottles with the usual hard bits on the bottle's neck. More like a greasy spoon than a cafe.

'So, what's this exciting news you have for us?' asked Steven.

'You'll not believe what I got through sheer luck and a little help from a friend,' Gary sounded animated.

'I'm not long out of bed, mate. I can't fucking think. Just spill the beans, eh?' Steven screwed up his face.

'Full access to the BBC Studios!' Steven and Donna sat with their mouths wide open in astonishment.

'What are you planning to do with that access? Burn the place down would be the right thing to do.' Donna's comment amused Chelsea.

'This is bigger and better than any fire, Donna,' she said.

'Global fucking headlines, my dear friends.'

Gary sat back in his chair with his hands clasped behind his head and continued to share the details of what Kevin had told him the night before. Steven and Donna's levels of excitement were rising. They both realised that this could be a once in a lifetime to make the changes they wanted. To make a difference in society. They were targeting a corporation that is known across the world.

'It makes me thrilled but nervous, but I should be used to that by now.' Donna chuckled. 'What about an escape plan?'

'This is where we need to change the number of people we want to be involved. We need to get back on the forum and get as many people as possible as a distraction,' said Gary.

'You have seen those flash dance videos, right?' Chelsea asked Donna.

'Yes, they are amazing.'

'That is our escape plan.' Gary looked at Steven and Donna.

Initially, they were confused, but by the time an hour had passed, they understood the plan. It was simple enough, but they needed more work and a back-up plan. It was OK getting a few security lads on your side, but with the BBC employees themselves, it would only take one to call the police. This is where the flash crowd would come in.

There were many bars, coffee shops, and restaurants around the BBC headquarters. The plan was for as many people as possible to book tables, be in pubs, get coffee, stand around the streets, but not in huge numbers. This would not be an organised protest. This was a flash crowd getaway.

If they could get a few hundred people in the area at a specific time, it would give them a crowd to escape into. The gathering would also stop the police from entering through the main door. It would be a bit like the ending of Escape to Victory, where the prisoners played the Germans at football, and after a victory, they escaped by being hidden within the crowd after a pitch invasion.

'How many do you think will join us?' Donna asked.

'It's difficult to say. It's been a while since I spent much time online,' Gary told her. 'I think there are five hundred in the south of England. Maybe two hundred locally.'

'I suggest we get back on the forums and inform people of a stunt on a global scale. That will gather more support. If we make this out as the biggest thing we have done to date, people will want to be part of it.' Steven rattled his fists on the table in anticipation and looked at Donna.

'Yes, I agree. This will take time, and we need to see what support we have,' she said.

'We also need people for the back-up plan, just in case we get some wannabe heroes from the BBC staff,' Chelsea suggested.

'We've got that covered with a few guys I know.' Gary sounded positive.

They discussed many scenarios and back-up plans for back-up plans. They were preparing for the most significant thing any of them ever imagined they would be involved in, but wanted to remain cautious. They also talked about the possibility of getting arrested and the consequences.

'If we get caught, everyone will know our names. We will be famous for a short while, so use that fifteen minutes of fame to our advantage. It's even more publicity!' Steven raised his eyebrows.

'Let's remain positive and don't think of getting caught. If it happens, then we deal with it then. Just remember why we are doing this.' Gary was optimistic.

The plan was simple on paper. Enter the BBC studios and make their way to the studio, broadcasting live. They would then head for the production studio and threaten the producer. He had to remain on the air, and should he cut the live broadcast, there would be consequences for their families.

The group would show them live video footage of another person in a clown mask at the front door of their homes via video calls. Kevin would have provided lists of potential troublemakers' addresses. It couldn't fail. Andy and Brad would remain at the production office, and the others would make their way in front of the cameras with their message for the British public. Yes, it was all simple on paper.

When they entered the BBC studio, crowds from the nearby cafes, restaurants, bars, and standing around the streets would make their way to the main entrance, creating a flash mob. This would catch the BBC security off guard and delay the response time of the police arriving at the main entrance, should someone call them.

They would disguise this as a protest to abolish the illegal TV licenses they forced many Brits to pay. Many people all over the UK had cancelled what saw as an unfair tax. Things were so desperate that the BBC announced they would invest one hundred and forty million pounds into catching people with no license; a total disgrace. The public are aware that they will continue to target vulnerable people, like pensioners and single mothers. The latter is a tactic they have used for decades; single mothers have more to worry about than financing a license.

They also ruled out making the fake protest public, as that would only give the BBC a tip-off and police would be in attendance before the planned time.

'What you making for dinner tonight?' Chelsea asked Steven.

'Beer and spirits!' He winked at her. 'If there's a lot of people coming, can I suggest we get a takeaway, and just have a buffet with beers?'

'There will be us four, Brad, Kevin and Andy, I think. They have still to confirm,' said Gary.

'Beer and buffet, it is then.'

Later that evening, everyone gathered at Steven's flat. They had enough Chinese food to feed them all and then again for lunch the next day; as Steven said, it's better to get too much than not enough. The fridge was so full of alcohol that some cider sat on the kitchen floor. They were having a great time chatting; sitting in a circle and involved in the same conversation. This was unusual after a few beers, as people tended to split into smaller groups. The girls talking about their own topics and guys talking football. This time, they were all the one team.

'Let's raise a glass, folks! To change the world,' Gary slurred his words.

They raised their cans and glasses towards the ceiling.

'To changing the world!' With shouts and smiles, the group bonded.

'We can be heroes, just for one day, we can be us, just for one day,' Steven sang the lyrics of David Bowie's 1977 song, Heroes.

'I think we should get the ball rolling now,' Gary changed the topic. 'Shall we spend half an hour in the forums to get the feeling of this just now, and then we will have a better idea tomorrow? It's almost the weekend. There's more chance of getting people online now than on a Friday or Saturday.'

'That's a good shout, Gary. Let's do it.' replied Steven.

He took his laptop from his rucksack as Gary walked towards his PC. The others didn't have their devices, so they stood over them, watching what was going on. Gary went into one forum and Steven another. They both posted the same message with the headline, *Urgent Help required – London Area,* with the following statement and Steven posting on behalf of Midnight Justice.

Good evening all,

My apologies for not being here as often as I would like to be, but the rat race that is life has kept me very busy. I have been involved in a few stunts that some of you may have read about in recent months, so that is partially why I've been absent.

Don't take my silence for inaction. I have been swamped and still appreciate all your efforts, no matter how small they may be.

I have another operation planned and need the assistance of as many people as possible that are based or can travel to London, two weeks on Thursday, at seven in the evening. This is not to be missed, as we expect this to have global headlines. There will be no violence involved, and everyone will act as a human shield, preventing the police from entering a building.

This operation shall be organised as a flash protest, and everyone should stay away from the location until exactly nineteen hundred hours. There are plenty of bars and restaurants minutes from the site, so maybe book a table and make sure you are finished with your meal for six fifty-five. It is paramount that everyone stays out of sight.

If you can make it along and give us the help we need, I would be very grateful. We are all fighting the exact cause against government corruption, to name but one. Let's all stand together and show them we, the people, have the power.

Leave your comments below, and I will get back with further details in the next couple of days.

Love and Peace.

Midnight Justice. - The People for The People. xx

'That's fucking tremendous, Gary.' Donna complimented him.

'Will you be changing your name to Seven o'clock, Justice?' Andy's joke made folk laugh.

'That's a shout for help. People can't ignore that, especially from Midnight Justice. I know of at least forty from there who will get involved just because it's Midnight Justice.' Kevin told them.

'Well, between the two forums, there's almost nine hundred online. Let's see how it goes tomorrow.' Gary got up and walked into the kitchen to get more drinks.

'Who's for a game of UNO?' asked Chelsea.

They attempted to switch off, relax, and enjoy their evening. It was important to black out, just for a short time, before the biggest and most dangerous operation of their lives.

Chapter 18

There was no hangover in sight, a surprise considering the amount of alcohol, including tequila, they had consumed. Many people refuse Tequila until they get past that specific intoxicated state when they say, 'Fuck it.' Everyone had felt great and was in good spirits. Donna, Chelsea and Gary even made it to work, while Steven said, 'Fuck it,' again.

He had sat up watching Money Heist on Netflix. There were a few more episodes to go before he was to meet Donna, so they would watch the rest together. Steven had another lazy day and did nothing really constructive. He had to cook dinner later for Donna but, while lying on the couch, he received a message from Gary.

I hope you're hangover free mate, check the forum, with a few smiley emojis.

'This can only be a good thing,' thought Steven, as he grabbed his laptop from his rucksack that he hadn't unpacked the night before.

He logged on to the forum and saw Midnight Justice's post was at eleven thousand views.

'This is incredible,' he thought.

He clicked on the link, and there were sixty-nine pages with fifty comments per page. 'Absolutely incredible!' He shouted as he punched both hands in the air as if he had just scored a goal.

His own post in the other forum had only four replies, as someone had posted a link to Midnight's original post, so nobody cared what Steven thought when Gary was online, but this wasn't a big deal. The message was out there, and that was the most important thing. The number of replies was in the thousands and still rising as Steven worked his way through the responses.

'I'm in great shape. Out-fucking-standing,' Steven's thoughts were extremely positive. He got comfortable on the couch and continued through the posts. Most of the posts pleased him. Not one post was negative towards their actions, whatever they were. People didn't know but were supportive anyway because Midnight Justice was involved. The only negativity was from people who had expressed their disappointment at not making it on the night. Steven thought to himself that even if only fifty percent of these people turned up for their next stunt, then it would be a success.

A few minutes later, Gary called from the office.

'Are you coming out for a beer or cider?' he asked Steven.

'Are you fucking serious, mate?'

'Why the fuck not? Get a grip on yourself and stop being so fucking sensible.'

'Not sure if I can be bothered if I'm honest, mate,' Steven sounded rough.

'Give yourself a fucking shake, take a shower, and move. I'm not taking no for an answer. See you in The Fox Bar in an hour, you fucking wimp. Bring your missus as Chelsea is coming too'

Before Steven had time to reply, Gary hung up the phone.

He thought about it and decided that Gary was right. A shower and get to fuck out of the flat, but only after reading more comments.

Count six mates and me, in.

I'm there 100%, was another comment.

I can organise a bus from Kent. A fifty-five-seater full. Not a problem, said user Never Trouble.

It was music to Steven's ears. He couldn't wait to tell the others and got ready in no time. On his way to The Fox Bar, there was something he wanted to do. He got a taxi, went directly to the florist. He bought some flowers for Donna. The taxi driver dropped him at the pub, then he paid the driver to deliver the flowers to Donna at her work. He left a message inside the flowers, saying, *Have a lovely day, honey. Get a taxi to The Fox Bar when you finish. Love you lots. Steven xxx*

Gary was still in the office. He felt on top of the world with all the replies he had been reading most of the morning. As usual, not much work got done, and it was all about appearance money. He could just blag his way through the shift if he wanted to, but nobody really cared what he had done. He just had to wait the final fifteen minutes to complete the entire five-hour shift, so he called Chelsea.

'I've got a problem; it's massive!' said a stressed sounding Gary down the phone.

'What's up, Gary? Are you OK?'

'I'm not sure. I've let someone down.'

'Can I do anything?'

'Well, you could meet them. If they are ordering anything, say yes on my behalf and just explain that I'm delayed a few minutes,' replied Gary, trying to hold back the laughter.

'Who are you going to meet, and what are you ordering?' Chelsea was concerned.

'Eh! I'm meeting Steven and Donna down at The Fox Bar, and I'm ordering a pint. Are you coming?'

'You funny bastard!'

'Make your way down, honey. I'll be there shortly. Love you!'

Carrying her bouquet, Donna arrived at The Fox Bar. By the time she got there, the others were on their third pints of cider. She was now playing catch up, so she asked for a tequila to accompany her cider.

'Your flowers are gorgeous, honey.' Chelsea hugged Donna.

'Thank you!'

Donna gave Steven a hug, a kiss, and another thank you.

'Where're my flowers? You're a miserable heartless bastard!' Chelsea looked towards Gary to make sure he knew she was joking.

'Well, here we go again. We're becoming right alcoholics.' Donna pointed towards the bar.

'Alcoholics go to meetings; we go to social gatherings,' Steven whispered as he went to the bar to get Donna her two drinks.

It was true. They met regularly and drank more than any of them had done in the last few years. They were enjoying their new, more sociable lives and friendships. The bills were getting paid, and nobody was getting hurt, so where was the problem? They sat around the table and chatted shit for the next hour. They kept all the discussions about the plan quiet until Andy, Brad, and Kevin arrived.

Kevin was the last to arrive because of the traffic and the stupid shift hours requested by the BBC. He took a seat between Andy and Brad, and it was down to business.

'I have the cards,' he said.

'Already! That didn't take long. How long will it take you to get the required information on them? I can get the card reader whenever I want,' said Gary.

'I have the cards,' repeated Kevin with a nod of the head.

'What, *the* cards?' Gary realised Kevin had the completed cards.

'I have eight cards with A1 security clearance all set up and ready to go. They are not active yet, as the date is too far away. We update the cards every four days, so nobody will notice for another four days when I activate them on the day. I don't need your card reader. Stick it up your arse!' Kevin pointed mockingly at Gary.

'I fucking love you, lad. What a fucking result. How the fuck did you manage that?' Steven was stunned.

'They asked me to check a few things in a certain area, and they were just lying there. I picked up a bundle in a panic, and I was lucky enough to grab eight. After leaving the area, I hacked into Alan Simpson's account. He's chief of security and is only one of the few directly employed by the BBC. A cunt of a man. So, if there's an enquiry after the day in question, it will look like he has issued them,' explained Kevin.

'I'm getting fed up with these celebrations; I'm becoming an alcoholic through celebrations!' Andy looked at his cider.

'Well done, Kevin,' said Brad, as he raised his glass in the air and asked the others to toast Kevin.

The importance of their roles was becoming more apparent to everyone. Also, what they had to do to make things run like a well-oiled machine. Six of them. Steven, Donna, Gary, Chelsea, Andy and Brad would be the only ones entering the building. Kevin had done his part with the passes, as well as all the information the group required, which included names, addresses, telephone numbers, even photos of who would work that night.

The clown masks were the choice everyone agreed on, but not the face masks they had previously used; this time, they would use rubber masks pulled over their heads. Holes cut out at the eyes would not reduce their vision too much. They also agreed to wear red coveralls because they were huge fans of the Netflix series, Money Heist. A fake company name on the coveralls would confuse people in the building, even for a few more seconds. 4TP Telecoms was the phoney company. It made sense if they wanted the group to get more recognition.

Gary took out his laptop from his rucksack.

'I think it's time to let the people know what we are doing, and then they can decide if they want to take part. The detail of the show is going to be posted now.'

'I'm bursting with excitement. It's going to be fucking mental. I'm going to make sure I'm nearby when it all goes down,' laughed Kevin as he took the laptop from Gary.

He had always dreamed of being involved in something like this.

Good afternoon, everyone. I hope you feel positive and energised because the people of the UK need you. On Thursday, the seventeenth, we will pull off the most daring stunt we never imagined could happen, but we need your support.

We plan to take over the BBC television centre while they are live on air. Our aim is to broadcast a message for the people, by the people. We want to tell the world that we will no longer sit back and watch the rich get richer and the poor get poorer. It's time we took a stand.

We have seen protest after protest over my lifetime and your own, but few seem to have produced results, so we need bigger and better. We need to address the nation and expose the MPs and journalists for who they really are. We are sick of them and us in our society.

The reality is they don't give a fuck about anyone other than themselves once they have established power. Corruption at the highest level is one of many points that will be emphasised. We urge the people of the United Kingdom to take to the streets at their local Government MP's office up and down the length and breadth of the UK the following weekend. We want this to be the biggest protest the country has ever seen. Men, women and children, all with the same beliefs, create a carnival atmosphere to help take back our lives and leave the life of misery that many have suffered too long behind us.

There has been very little progress over the last decade due to austerity caused by bankers. These bankers were never in court and have never seen a prison. Why?

When The One Show starts on Thursday, we will enter the studio. We will then send out our message. We have methods to ensure they will not take us off the air. We estimate that, should everything go to plan, our statement shall take no longer than three minutes. This is where you come in.

We need everyone to be in the surrounding areas, whether in a bar, a coffee shop or a restaurant, just don't gather in large crowds in the nearby streets, as that will only draw attention. There are plenty of establishments around the area to eat and drink. At five minutes before seven pm, everyone should make their way to the main entrance of the BBC studio and block the direct access. This will be our very own flash mob.

I would request that everyone take a bag with, if possible, red coveralls and a clown mask to be worn before you arrive at the entrance. By the time you arrive at the location, we will already be in the building and putting our plan into action. We will confirm this by telephone with some people who will be outside. You are our escape plan. The team involved and I will disappear into the crowd, and we will walk away from the building altogether. Remember the ending from Escape to Victory?

Anyone with questions or wishes for more information can leave a message here, and I will gladly go through and answer as many as possible over the next few days.

I hope you will join us and be part of an evening that will go down in history. Please keep this within the group or with people you can trust.

Peace and love.

Midnight Justice. TPFTP xx

Kevin read it out loud as the others sat in silence.

'Wow! That is fucking awesome,' said Donna.

'That is just amazing,' said an even more excited Kevin.

'I love it,' commented Chelsea, and gave Gary a high five.

'This is what we got into this for. If we don't take risks, we don't have a chance of winning prizes. That's brilliant, mate,' said Steven.

Over the next hour, they sat drinking and discussed their plans and who would do what. Everyone was told to go over their roles as often as possible, even if it meant standing in front of the bathroom mirror rehearsing. It needed to be precise and to the script.

Chapter 19

The seventeenth of the month had arrived. Steven, Donna, Gary and Chelsea took the day off from work. All four were excited but shitting themselves.

Gary and Chelsea stayed over at Steven's flat the night before. They were not drinking alcohol; tea or coffee was the strongest drink on offer. In full concentration mode, they went over every delicate detail. Everyone had plenty of time to practise, and that's precisely what they did. They were about to take part in the most significant event in their lives to date.

Gary and Steven woke up just after six that morning and responded to posts in the forum. The support that they created gave them the adrenalin needed to keep going. If the information was correct and people were truthful, thousands would turn up on the evening in question. People were bringing friends, and at least eleven buses were coming from other areas as far away as Liverpool.

People felt strongly about the BBC event and saw this as a tremendous opportunity not to be missed.

'Have you seen this post?' Steven pointed to his laptop screen.

'No, what's it about?'

'This guy said he has a box of twenty-four red smoke bombs that he's bringing for when we leave the building.'

'That's the spirit; these could come in very handy on our exit. Tell him to keep them for when we leave the building.'

Steven posted the reply, instructing the member not to let them off until after the six of them were back on the street and mixing with the crowd.

The rest of their day seemed to drag in, slower than a week in prison, Gary pointed out, even though he could only imagine a week behind bars would drag. The women woke up just after eight. Over breakfast at the dining room table, they discussed what could go wrong. They didn't care about the consequence anymore. It had gone too far. They had agreed.

'Fuck it. What will be, will be.'

There was tension in the air, and overthinking meant they were quieter than usual. There wasn't much conversation, only music in the background. Most of the morning, even when preparing coveralls and clown masks, they were deep in their own thoughts.

'Do my eyes look enormous in this?' Donna broke the nervous silence as she slipped the clown mask over her head and looked at Chelsea.

'Can you see around, OK?'

'Yes, cutting the eyes bigger sure makes a difference, but don't make the holes too big, remember?'

They prepared with care and made sure they had everything that would be necessary. The only thing that remained was to double-check they had one hundred percent battery life in their phones. This was extremely important. Time ticked by. It was almost time for them to set out for the BBC studios. The plan was to make their own way there using public transport and keep their heads covered with hoodies. They arranged a meeting point down a small alleyway only seventy-five metres from the main BBC entrance. That is where they would change into the coveralls and masks.

Donna and Steven took the bus, but didn't sit together. Gary and Chelsea drove home first and took a different bus route, again not sitting together. Brad and Andy also made their way on public transport. They had agreed to meet at the back door of a closed-down restaurant, which would give them cover to change into their disguise. It came to eighteen forty-seven that evening, and everyone was in place.

'Does everyone have their phones at hand?' Gary spoke through the rubber clown mask and wore his red coveralls.

'Check,' the other five said, one after another.

'If anyone feels they want to back out, this is the time to say so. There will be no hard feelings, and we'll all still be friends,' said Gary.

Everyone was silent.

'I'm in this for the memory of old Stanley and the thousands of others like him,' said Steven.

'Me too.'

'Let's do this.'

'We can do this.'

'We're going to make global headlines tonight.'

'We are the people fighting for the people.'

Each said their piece.

'We are not terrorists, we are not anarchists, we are just ordinary people who are fed up with the lies and bullshit fed to us by our government and the mainstream media. We will now tell them we're not putting up with this shit anymore,' ranted Gary in a voice that just oozed leadership as they had a group hug.

It was time for them to begin. The studio was on the second floor, on the northern face of the building. Gary and Steven pulled a small banner from their rucksacks that read, 'Abolish the BBC TV licence.' They approached the building. This was to throw people off the scent, especially the security. Who would think they are just a couple of nutters with nothing else to do on a Thursday evening?

As they arrived at the main entrance, it was one minute to seven. It was now or never.

'BBC license is an illegal tax,' shouted Steven repetitively, and just as expected, the solo security guard arrived at the door.

'You can't be here. If you want to protest, move to the other side of the car park. You are on private property here,' he informed the group.

Five of the group stood shouting anti-BBC abuse whilst Brad went through his phone. Within seconds, he turned around to the guard and was right in his face.

'Robert, you are almost forty years old. You don't get paid enough for this, so let's not be silly. Be a good boy and move out of the way.'

'You need to move from here before I call for backup and the police,' the guard continued.

'Robert, listen carefully. We will be going inside in ten seconds. Don't call the police. Our friends are at your house right now.'

'Do you want your wife's car destroyed? And all your windows?' Gary asked in an angry, authoritative tone.

Andy had taken a picture of Robert's semi-detached house with his wife's car in the driveway. Robert's face dropped when he saw it. In a state of shock, he stood out of the way, giving the group the green light to enter the building.

'Remember Robert. As it stands now, you are the only one who knows we are here. Should the police arrive, it's only one phone call to the people standing outside your house, and the destruction will scar your wife and young daughter for the rest of their lives. Have a seat over there.' Gary pointed to a bench as he walked past Robert.

The group proceeded to the elevators with the now-activated passes in hand. Up to the second floor, take a right, and the studio would be directly in front of them. Brad and Andy were last in the elevator, and first out, so they headed to the production control room. The others went directly into the studio and stood at the doors to keep an eye out. Andy swiped his security pass and, to his relief, the door of the production control room opened.

'Everyone, stay where you are!' Brad yelled.

'What's going on here? Someone call security!' said the grey-haired man in a posh accent.

He reminded Brad of an older-looking James May who previously worked for the BBC on Top Gear.

'Not so fucking fast. You will listen to us, and this show will remain on air. There will be severe consequences for the families of everyone in this room if this plan doesn't go ahead.' Brad said menacingly.

'We have your names and addresses; people are standing outside your homes as we speak. Your families are in danger if you don't do what you are told!' Andy shouted.

At that, one of the control room team picked up the phone.

'Fuck you, I'm calling security,'

Brad began reading out the names and addresses of the people in the room. By the look on the face of the want to be the hero controller, his name was read out first. He put the phone down.

'We know you all, and time is ticking. We only ask you to keep this show on the air. Look at this, Mr Richardson.' Brad held his phone in front of the show's producer.

'We are here outside your fancy home and might poison your dogs before we destroy the place, you fucking posh bastard!' The voice on the other end of the phone screamed.

'We currently have people outside your homes; it's up to you how this goes from now on,' said Andy. 'Inform the cameramen and the rest of your team, including the presenters, exactly what is happening. We don't want any heroics live on TV. We are not here to harm anyone, but only to deliver a message to the British people. In three minutes, we will be gone.

Brad had his phone in hand and sent a WhatsApp message simply saying, *Go, go,* to Steven and Gary, who told Donna and Chelsea to enter first and walk towards the audience and presenters. The audience didn't seem to know what was happening, and stood in silence, thinking it was part of the show. Gary and Steven followed behind their other halves.

'Presenters! Please take a seat to the side. We will be gone in three minutes,' Donna said in a nervous voice.

The control room informed the presenters via their earpiece and did as they were told. Because the show was still on the air and the presenters, camera crew, and others were doing nothing, the small audience did the same, totally oblivious to what was happening. Donna set the stopwatch on her phone. It would count down three minutes from the exact moment Gary started speaking.

Gary and Steven stood behind the couch in the centre. Donna and Chelsea stood at either end of the couch. What had been once a dream was now a reality. The four of them were now live, in front of an audience of millions. It was showtime!

'We are from a group named The People For The People. We are not a terrorist organisation, we are not a Marxist organisation, we are ordinary people like most of the UK. Today, we are sending a message to the UK Government and the mainstream media. That message is we will not tolerate your corruption, austerity, fraud, and media bias. The officials and media can spin this whatever way they like, but we are the voice of the people. We have massive numbers and are still growing by the hour.

Our nation, according to many, is one of the wealthiest countries in the world. So why is there still so much poverty? Why is there so much homelessness? Why are our ex-servicemen living on the streets?' Gary looked towards camera number three, directly in front of him, just as he indicated Steven should take over.

'Why have we been led to believe we need austerity to recover from something that none of us is responsible for? Ask yourself this. How many bankers have been in court? None, I tell you! If we look at the small and beautiful nation of Iceland. Their courts sentenced thirty-six bankers to ninety-six years in prison.

All the criminal cases are linked to the notorious crash of the Icelandic banking system in 2008, which we are still paying for today. How many have been to prison in the UK? None, I tell you! How many MPs are found to be fiddling expenses? Apologise, pay it back, and that is the end. If this was a hungry person stealing from a supermarket continuously, he would be in prison.' Steven finished his rant, so Gary took over.

'In this country, we seem to sit back and take whatever is thrown at us. People say that it's the great British spirit that we have when the reality is we don't have any fucking choice. Do the French sit back like us? No, they don't. Over the last few decades, we have had bankers' bailouts, cuts to emergency services, and many fire stations closed down. Yet, MPs continue to get an above-inflation pay raise each year, even if they don't deserve it, all while NHS staff are working more hours than should be legal just to survive,' shouted Gary.

Much to his surprise, a few members of the audience applauded.

'We have older women robbed of pensions. We have the third-lowest pension payments in the western world. Why did we give money to countries like Pakistan who financed a nuclear weapons programme? Why do we give India, another nuclear weapons nation, one billion pounds, then they spent three hundred and thirty million on a statue? Why are we giving over three hundred million to the likes of Nigeria, who has one of the most corrupt governments on the planet? How could anyone justify giving away over thirteen billion in total when, I repeat, ex-servicemen are sleeping on our own streets?

We call for more transparency into overseas aid and think the public should know exactly what we get in return. Charity begins at home. Our police forces are now more of a business, as meeting targets is more important than catching criminals. There are laws for MPs and laws for us, it seems. The police force across the UK has become a vehicle for political correctness.' Gary finished.

During this part of the speech, Donna texted Andy to ask if everything was OK in the production room. He told her things were under control and everyone was silently watching.

'We don't have much time left, but we need to take a stand against governments and the mainstream media. The BBC is nothing more than a leftist propaganda machine and is getting too big for its boots. There is nothing impartial about this organisation.

I urge each of you to stop paying for the TV license. It's an outdated criminalising TAX. The BBC's most significant targets are single mothers and the older generation, with tactics that spread fear. It's time to abolish the license,' said an emotional Gary.

'Who remembers the days when journalists did journalistic things? They looked for stories and reported them in the public's interest. Nowadays, many stories are avoided by the mainstream media. The cover-ups are happening daily, not by all newspapers and TV, but by the majority. Stop buying them and stop clicking on their websites.' Gary looked for Steven to take over the speech.

'We have seen ordinary people have the choice of eating or heating. I know of someone who paid tax all his life and died of hypothermia because he ate *and* wore clothes. Is this the reality of 2020? Many people abroad would love to come to our country as they see the dream of living in one of the world's most incredible places, but it's all a myth. We can't look after our own, and the MPs that we vote in don't really give a fuck about us. It's only their salary they care about.

The last time Parliament had every MP in attendance was to debate their own pay rise. Is this acceptable to the people of Great Britain and Northern Ireland? Only eight percent turned up and bothered voting when it came to the debate on our excellent NHS staff's pay increase. Do you see the problem?

We don't need to accept this. We are a peaceful organisation that has simply had enough. Will you join us? Help us uncover governmental and media cover-ups and fraud that happen daily. Remember that these MPs work for you, so make them work for their excessive salaries,' shouted Steven, as he let Gary take over once again.

'We will be back in touch with the public, but for now, we call on every man, woman and child to begin their fight back by protesting two weeks on Saturday at their local authority or government building. We shall never be defeated, we shall never surrender, as long as we stick together and disregard the government's conquer and divide tactics, which have been used since the days of the Roman Empire. We are The People For The People. Thank you so much for your attention. Goodnight.'

The four of them calmly walked off the stage, although they were shaking inside.

⦿⟨⟩⦿

Chapter 20

A staff member at one of the local restaurants wondered what had happened that night. It was never that busy, especially around five forty-five in the evening. He asked some customers what they had planned that evening, and almost everyone gave the same reasons. 'Nothing special, we just fancied somewhere different,' or 'It's someone's birthday.' There was nothing strange about their reasons, but to have every table full so early in the evening was crazy, especially as the majority were walk-ins. By comparison, the restaurant was only that busy around eight o'clock on a Saturday.

It wasn't just restaurants that were busy. The entire area was buzzing. Bars, coffee shops, McDonald's, Kentucky Fried Chicken and Pizza Hut. People were standing outside bars in some areas, as there was no room inside. But all this changed at six-fifty. Waitresses and waiters were rushing around trying not to screw up their tips by getting bills to everyone on request. It was like everyone had to be somewhere within the next few minutes as their moods went from being very relaxed to in a hurry. Maybe there was some music concert on. The area was back to the same volume of customers as most Thursdays in no time. Quiet.

It was around five minutes to seven, and as people left local businesses, it was like the scene from a football match, with fans slowly walking towards the stadium where their team was playing. It was an enormous crowd, and it mesmerised many locals.

People had come from all directions, and within minutes, about seven thousand people stood at the main entrance to the BBC. Most changed clothes as they got to the car park entrance. It was a sea of red clothing and clown masks.

People were shouting, 'Defund the B-B-C,' and clapping. It was an anti-license fee protest to anyone walking by, unaware of the unfolding drama.

Robert, the security guard, was out of his comfort zone. He was in a panic, pacing up and down inside the main entrance, sweating profusely and watching thousands hurl abuse at his employers. Putting two and two together, he concluded they were all in this together. This was part of their plan, so he refrained from calling the police; he was worried about the people outside his home. He couldn't help thinking about what was going on upstairs; why had nobody from the studio called for any help? He pulled out his phone and began streaming BBC One Live to give him a hint of what was going on. He caught the last thirty seconds of Steven's speech and watched them disappear from the screen, then pan back to the presenters, who apologised and said they would be back tomorrow. The BBC cut to an old episode of The Antiques Roadshow.

'Where are they now?' he thought.

Again, he convinced himself not to call the police.

'That wasn't so hard now, was it, Robert?' said Gary as he stepped out of the elevator.

'Are they all with you?' asked Robert.

'This is the people, Robert. Maybe you can join us one day and leave this horrible organisation behind you. And just to make you feel better, we know where you live, but there was nobody at your home, and nothing would have happened to your house, family or car,' Gary. assured him. 'You see, Robert, we are decent people fighting for what I think you also believe in. We try to do our work without anyone getting injured.'

'Enough of the chit-chat Gary, let's move,' Steven shouted, as he looked out to the main entrance.

In front of him was a sea of red and various styles of clown masks. The sound of police sirens screamed in the background.

'Take a few seconds here,' Gary addressed the rest of the group. 'Let's soak this up and enjoy it.'

'Have you fucking lost the plot?' asked Donna, as she looked through the glass doors to the enormous crowd.

They stood at the entrance watching everyone shout abuse and some people urging them to come out of the building, but this was their moment. They wanted to create memories and soak up what they achieved in getting everyone at the location.

'Right, that's fucking long enough. Let's go!' Chelsea snapped the others out of their trance.

The group left through the main doors and, at the back of the massive crowd, they saw around six or seven police cars attempting to get closer. Officers on foot were trying to pass through, but the crowd stood firm and held them back by linking arms and forming a chain across the entire entrance.

When the group exited the BBC building, there was a massive cheer as they joined the thousands of people. It was a moment none of them would ever forget. It was their heroic moment; their Escape to Victory moment. It was not something they expected to be so easy, so it took them by surprise.

'We are the people, we are the people, we are the people,' chanted the crowd as they surrounded the group, patting them on the head and back with huge smiles behind their masks.

'Fucking legends,' shouted a few of the crowd.

Within seconds, the crowd pushed them into the middle of the throng, away from the entrance. It was now impossible for them to be identified. They struggled to see each other through the denseness of the smoke bombs that filled the area with a thick red cloud. Sometimes they couldn't see what direction they were walking in, as they were being pushed around, but had faith in their own supporters to escort them to safety.

'Watching all the re-runs of Escape to Victory has its advantages, eh?' Steven called out.

They struggled to hold on to each other's clothing in the centre of what was a protective circle of people around them, just like in the 1981 movie, where the prisoners of war were escorted out of the football stadium in Germany after beating the Germans on their own patch.

'This is fucking incredible!' Gary's shouts were weak over the continuous chants of, 'We are the people,' and 'Defund the B-B-C.'

Donna and Chelsea were silent. Both enjoyed every minute and by then had their phones in the air, capturing the footage to look back on and share online later.

On the junction of the main road, police gathered in more significant numbers, but the crowd pushed them aside and created a space that enabled them to stream out back onto the main road. They were free. The job was done. It was a massive sigh of relief for everyone involved. It was only a matter of getting back to the flat now.

They walked amongst the crowd for around a quarter of a mile, with the police following behind. Many people removed their masks and found their own routes, splitting the public into many sections as planned.

A few minutes later, the police realised this and stopped following them. They had no suspects; there was no violence, although they had the video camera in hand to study at a later date for potential suspects.

'Down here, let's go,' Gary instructed the others.

'That was, without doubt, the most incredible thing I have ever done in my life.' Chelsea was shaking uncontrollably.

'Me too, honey.' Donna clapped her hands.

'Let's get these coveralls off and back to my place for a celebration.'

Steven helped Donna with the shoulder of her tightly fitted coveralls.

'I could really do with a few tonight while we follow the aftermath on the TV,' Gary admitted.

'It's going to be epic, mate. Global headlines, I suspect.' Steven was grinning.

They got changed and ditched the coveralls and masks in a nearby bin. Gary took out his lighter and grabbed some oversized boxes sitting at the side. They ripped them up and set fire to the bin. The container was ablaze within a couple of minutes; their coveralls and masks joined the dancing flames.

Some of the crowd went their own way, but there were still thousands hanging around the area. Clown masks littered the pavements, coveralls, and the odd red Liverpool football shirt hung over fences. Pubs were bustling again, and everyone talked about what had just happened. The internet was on fire, especially Twitter and YouTube, where people posted footage of the three-minute speech of The One Show. People were watching it repeatedly. #theoneshow and #thepeopleforthepeople were now trending in the UK.

Media across the world couldn't believe what had just happened. There were tweets from South Korea, New Zealand, the USA, Australia. Everyone was talking about the biggest publicity stunt ever seen in the UK. But the most important thing was, they loved it.

'Are the little people fighting back?' That was the question everyone asked.

Was it time to change the political setup in the UK?

The six of them made their way back to Steven's flat. Every one of them buzzing with excitement. It was their moment. Steven went directly to the fridge and pulled out two bottles of champagne.

'No cider just yet, people. We have celebrating to do.'

He pulled the foil top from the cork and twisted it open to see the cork fly across the room, just missing Brad's eye.

Chelsea sat at the dining table, placing her face flat on the table, and panting.

'Are you OK, honey?' asked Gary.

'Yeah, I'm fine. I'm in a bit of shock, to be honest. I think the reality of what has just happened is sinking in. You know our lives will never be the same, right?'

She picked her head up and took a glass of champagne from Gary.

'I want more adrenalin like that.' Steven's smile was infectious.

'It was the greatest feeling in the world, better than any drug, I would imagine.' Chelsea sighed.

Steven faced the kitchen window from the far end of the dining table so that he could see his five friends face to face.

'I just want to say a few words to each of you. From the morning Stanley died, I think that was when I changed as a man. My life changed to take another direction. Although the death of Stanley was sad, something good has come from it. If he hadn't died that morning, then when you think about it, we might never have crossed paths.'

'Is this going to be a record-breaking speech? I have work tomorrow morning.' Gary put his hands on his hips.

'In the short time that we have known each other, the bond between us has become strong, and we are all on the same page. Your friendship has been like a breath of fresh air in my life. Never in a million years did I think I would be involved in something so big. Our lives take a particular path, and I believe someone wrote them for us. It meant us to be together as a group. We have people out there who need our voice. Millions can't speak up, and when they do, there is nobody there to listen. We are their voice. We are the people, for the people, and I thank you all for being part of it,' Steven's voice was cracking.

The others cheered and walked over, one by one, to give Steven a hug. Others were emotional as they took Steven's words to heart. He was correct, though. The group had created a solid friendship, something many of them had missed from their lives. They all knew people here and there, more associates, but they had never had this strength of friendship, which only made them value it even more.

'Who wants to watch some TV?' Brad asked.

'Sky News anyone?' Andy finished his champagne and helped himself to a bottle of beer from the fridge.

'Where do we go from here?' Brad asked.

'The British public now know we exist. If we do too much, we could lose public support, so we need to keep calm and think about another publicity stunt, but not too soon. We first need to see how many people actually come to protest next Saturday. If there are only a few thousand here and there in major cities up and down the countries, then we need to keep at it. If there are many thousands, then we are halfway there.'

There was a mutual agreement.

'You are not going to fucking believe this guy,' Andy announced from the living room doorway.

He could not hide his exhilaration.

'World leaders are making comments about The One Show. Prime Ministers and Presidents are commenting around the fucking globe. We are global news!' said Andy, as he shook his bottle of beer and poured it all over his own head in a fit of laughter.

It was true. The Prime Minister of New Zealand called the stunt, 'The work of normal Joe Bloggs, the people.'

People standing up against the corruption of the Eton elite really excited the group. Totally unexpected but genuine.

The USA, Canada, the EU, Germany, France, and many others all gave their opinions, but there was still nothing from the UK Government. The BBC released a statement saying that the group was nothing more than domestic terrorists, which didn't go down well with the public on all social media platforms.

In fact, the statement possibly pushed anyone sitting on the fence against the BBC and Parliament. It was a PR disaster for everyone at the BBC.

'Did someone say party?' Kevin walked in the front door, hugging everyone and showing his delight with a massive grin on his face.

'You have nothing to worry about, guys. They don't have a clue. They have no leads, and as a small bonus to my friends. The video footage of you in the building and leaving has been, let's say, misplaced,' said Kevin.

He had been in the BBC building when everything happened and decided on a whim to delete the footage from the server.

'You fucking superstar,' said Donna, giving him another hug.

As the group celebrated for the rest of the night, the internet was still on fire. Many people were taking an interest. Some were asking why nobody had done something like this in their country? When will the average person rise and hold their politicians to account? There were many interesting conversations. Some were sensible, some really stupid. One topic that took hold of people's attention was the idea of having MPs reviewed by their constituency after a specific time frame. This would help eliminate the possibility of MPs going back on their promises before elections. Something many UK politicians were guilty of.

The group ignored all the comments and most of the media. They switched the TV and laptops off, put on some music, and partied into the small hours of Friday morning. A Friday was the start of their new lives; they were undercover heroes whose identity was only known only to a few people.

Chapter 21

'Good morning, and welcome to GMTV. Here are this morning's headlines,' said the female presenter on ITV.

Stephen opened his eyes. He felt the sudden pain in the front of his head when he moved. Someone had delivered his hangover.

'Good morning, mate.' Gary sat on a chair opposite, watching the TV.

'Help me, mate, I'm fucking almost dead here,' Steven groaned.

'We are global news, mate. The world is talking about us.'

Gary couldn't keep his mouth closed. His body was pumping with adrenaline, and he forgot about any hangover the others may be suffering. Although Chelsea and Donna were still sleeping in Steven's bed, they did not know about the latest developments.

'I have been watching this for over an hour; the people love us.'

Gary made coffee and spent the next forty minutes talking continuously, with minimal input from Steven. He spoke about the media's reaction, the forum's reaction, and even his own ideas on where to go with the next stunt.

The BBC tried its best to play down the story, but social media gave everyone the correct public opinion. Many members of the public wanted to know who these people were and wanted to join them. They were also The People and thought that the group represented them. They felt they had more of a connection after listening to the speech on The One Show.

In Australia, the Aussies in the forum made plans to carry out some similar stunts and attempted to gather more support to extend the size of their group. Folk repeated this in many countries across the world.

The forum had quadrupled in membership during the last twelve hours, and the servers struggled. Gary pointed out that twenty-eight countries now had their own sub-forums, compared to eight, only three weeks ago.

Although the groups had a severe dislike for most of the media, the Sun won the day and brought a smile to their faces. On the front page, they published a photograph of thousands of people in clown masks, walking away from the BBC building. The headline read, *Clowns take over the Circus*. It went against the grain of most UK and global media. They were still Scum, though.

'We need a holiday,' Steven suggested. 'We need to get away and just hang out.'

'You have a serious dose of the fears, my friend,' said Gary.

'Why don't we just get away for a week or two and chill? Nothing will be happening here for a while. We have no plans for anything else, and we need to let the dust settle.' Steven had finished his second coffee of the morning and was feeling a bit more alive.

'Have you been to Italy? I've always wanted to go there,' Gary told him.

They sat and discussed what to do next. Steven's chief concern was Donna getting into any trouble and he clarified she was his priority now. He would take any blame as long as she avoided any prison time. He wanted to protect her and would feel a lot safer in another country, where he wouldn't always be looking over his shoulder. Gary took the same line of thought in protecting Chelsea, and they agreed a break would be ideal. Just the four of them. Brad and Andy wouldn't have the funds.

Donna and Chelsea arrived in the living area. Donna rubbed her eyes, and Chelsea put her hands through her hair.

'Coffee in bed would have been nice, Steven!' Chelsea gave a cheeky smirk as she kissed Gary.

'I didn't want to wake you, honey.'

'Who likes pizza and strong coffee?' Gary asked.

'Only with pineapple, but not for breakfast.' Chelsea turned up her nose at the offer.

'I think that's illegal in Italy, shall we tell them?'

Much to the girls' delight, Steven and Gary suggested they go on holiday until things calmed down a bit in the media. Police or serious crime squad could knock on the door at six in the morning. It was also good for their mental health to switch off from everything, including the media. It removed any paranoia.

'Where shall we go?' Donna asked.

'How does a visit to the Amalfi coast sound?'

The girls jumped up and down, hugging each other.

Around twenty minutes later, the four sat in the living area and selected flights and a hotel in Salerno. They liked the name of The Grand Hotel and its location. It was a short walk from the main shopping area, with a sea view and a spa pool. Just what they needed. They booked a two-hour forty-minute flight to Salerno from Luton, London, the next day. Travel arrangements were made; all they required was to get packed.

They texted the following day and agreed to meet up at the airport early and have some lunch. Their flight was departing at three o'clock, so just after midday was ideal.

'Was it just me, or did anyone else notice the front pages of the newspapers in WH Smith's?' Steven asked the others.

'That was us; we were very naughty.' Chelsea slapped the back of her own hand.

Two days after the main event, the TV reports went into overdrive with some crazy bullshit; *The BBC should have armed guards. The people are domestic terrorists. When they are caught, it should be life sentences.* The newspapers had a different angle. It was as though they saw the power of the people and took a more supportive role. Headlines went along the lines of *Hold the MPs accountable. The Rise of Britain. British Public is sick of the same no matter who is elected.*

One newspaper went further than usual with the headline. *Born, Taxed, Dead – Is retirement a thing of the past?* They took the side of the people and asked why more and more people couldn't retire when they were of age. It was becoming more common that people were working in their seventies, more like the US, where they simply couldn't afford to give up working.

Worked to death, they called it. It was music to the group's ears. This was precisely why they did what they did. They didn't need every media outlet supporting them, just the one would do, which is exactly what happened. The Daily Star went against the grain of every other newspaper. They later announced that traffic to their website crashed the servers. The people saw what side the Daily Star was on and loved it.

'Pint of cider, anyone?' Gary asked as they took their seats in Frankie and Benny's, inside Luton Airport.

'Plenty of ice, mate,' Steven reminded him as he picked up the menu from the table.

After breakfast, they headed to the gate and boarded. The flight was over in no time.

'Welcome to Naples,' said a crew member.

They returned his greeting. After they had picked up their bags, they took a taxi to Naples central station; the train to Salerno lasted an hour and four minutes, followed by the eight-minute walk to the hotel.

'We'd better have a sea view,' Chelsea remarked.

She took in the architecture of the Italian buildings as they approached the hotel entrance.

'Good afternoon, four of us wish to check-in,' said Gary, as he handed over four passports.

'Buon pomeriggio. Good afternoon,' said the small, stunning-looking Italian woman at reception. Marilena was her name unless she was wearing another member of staff's Grand Hotel name tag on her blouse.

They chatted for a few minutes with Marilena, asking about the area and how to get places. As a hotel receptionist, she went above and beyond her duty. She told them about local restaurants and transport links to Amalfi and Pompeii for day trips. She was the perfect welcome to Italy, and now the group had all the information they needed within twenty minutes of arriving in Salerno.

They went to their rooms and agreed they would go out for food around seven that evening.

'What do you think of the hotel rooms?' Donna asked Chelsea, as they met later in the hotel lobby.

'They have average facilities, but they are massive.'

'At least we have a great view of the Med. It's just stunning.'

They walked to the main door and met Marilena just finishing her shift.

'Are you going to eat now?' she asked the group in her striking Italian accent.

'Yes, we're going to walk around and see what's out there. Maybe have a look on trip advisor,' replied Gary.

'There is a fantastic restaurant further down the street to the right. It has an outside terrace and shouldn't be too busy at this time. It's called Mondo Cibus. They will look after you.'

'Thank you. We'll have a look on the way.' Donna smiled.

Marilena had been a great help so far, so they took her advice and went to the restaurant, which had a few tables and chairs outside and was small inside. It was set in a pedestrian area surrounded by magnificent Italian buildings and other restaurants and was only fifty feet from the main shopping street. From arriving, the service was superb, and after a few red wines, the group ordered their food.

'Put your phone away,' Chelsea told Gary in a pretend angry voice.

'OK, OK, I was just checking the —— '

'The news!' Donna interrupted. 'We are here to get away from that and let our hair down. Do what you are told!'

It was at this point, Steven received a text message.

Check out the forum a.s.a.p!!!!!

'I need to burst the seal already. Where are the toilets in here?' Steven turned to the waiter who pointed to the back of the restaurant.

Steven went into a solo cubical and opened the forum.

One Show Suspects in Custody, four men arrested, was the main thread with thousands of replies.

Steven asked himself if this was good news or bad news. Good news if it would take the heat off them, especially Donna and Chelsea, but bad news, as he couldn't let someone else go to prison for something they didn't do.

'I did need to burst the seal, but I also needed to check a vital message on my phone and stop you two moaning,' Steven said, as he returned to his seat.

'Really important?' asked Donna.

Steven showed the rest of the group what he had just read, and they sat for a few minutes in silence. Their brains worked overtime. It wasn't just Steven who felt terrible; they all felt that someone taking the blame was not the right thing.

'What're your thoughts, Gary?' asked Chelsea.

'I'm not sure yet, but if the men didn't do it, they should be found not guilty, right?' said Gary.

'They will be remanded, without a doubt,' said Chelsea.

'We are in so deep, we never thought of this kind of scenario. Do we know who the guys are?' asked Donna.

'We can find out tomorrow and take it from there.' Gary took massive gulps of fine Italian red wine from the glass until it was done.

'Can we have another bottle of vino Rosso, per favore?' Gary used his Italian vocabulary to its maximum. It was from that moment on he had only one intention: to get drunk.

All four had a fantastic time in Italy. They travelled to Amalfi by bus through the craziest winding road they had ever been on, at one time thinking they were going over the edge of a cliff. All were happy that none of them were driving. They took the train to learn more about Pompeii and came back more educated than when they boarded their outbound flight.

'We would like to check out now, Marilena.' Steven handed the key fobs over the counter.

'Did you have a pleasant stay in Salerno?' she asked politely.

'We all had a great time. It's a beautiful place, and if it wasn't for your recommendations and advice, it wouldn't have been the same, so Grazie,' Donna added, as they said their goodbyes.

The short walk to the train station meant they caught the twelve-twenty train back to Naples, and then grabbed a taxi to the airport. They negotiated a fare on the way once they were in the cab. That seemed to be the way things worked in Naples.

There was a strange silence between them. Nobody knew what to expect on their return to London. They hadn't checked their phones and had completely switched their minds off for the last thirteen days to enjoy their holiday. They went totally off the radar in all forums, which was a good choice because if they had known what was going on, things in Steven's head would have been different.

Very different.

Chapter 22

After completing an intense four-day forklift course, Ryan Walker had secured a job within days. This was a new chapter in his life, a fresh start. Instead of repeating the pattern from his old life, lying in bed until late afternoon and then going shoplifting to fund his heroin habit, he was awake each day before his alarm and into a more enjoyable lifestyle.

When he wasn't on drugs, he was a friendly young man. He was not as shy as his brother, Steven. It suited Ryan's character to be more up front, and he liked to be around people when he was clean. Each day, he met more people in the warehouse, more than the whole time he had worked at his father's company. That wasn't surprising, as he'd only lasted a week before his father sacked him. After the petty cash went missing, they saw the evidence on CCTV, leaving no choice.

Although life was good, one issue was out of Ryan's control. Since starting his new job months ago, drug dealers reckoned he had surplus money and would go looking for him with offers of reduced-price heroin. He was tempted, but didn't want to let himself or Gemma down. It had been difficult enough for him to start again after he lost everything. He was determined not to go through that again.

'I'll do you buy two, get one free, mate,' explained John, his ex-close friend turned drug dealer.

'Fuck off. I'm not interested.'

Ryan attempted to walk in the opposite direction of the dealer, who was getting more persistent and aggressive while his two cronies looked on.

Ryan saw no let-up in being pressured into buying heroin. He felt a surge of rage that he had never felt before and quickly turned and grabbed John by the throat, throwing him against the closed shop's steel shutter, which created a considerable noise, drawing attention to the public. He held him against the shutter.

'Take your drugs and stick them up your fucking arse. I don't fucking want them. I don't fucking need them. Come near me again, and I will fucking destroy you.' Ryan let go of his grip.

'You fucked up, Ryan. Nobody does that to me and gets away with it. This isn't finished with.' John's stumble turned into a slow jog away from Ryan, and the two mates followed John like sheep.

Trouble was all Ryan needed after a long day at work. As he headed home, he thought back to the days at the height of his addiction with a smile, recognising how far he had come, and felt proud. Down the local drinking den, The Fox Bar, he had sold hundreds of pounds' worth of meat stolen from supermarkets. Even the bar staff jumped at the less than half-price steaks.

I've moved on. Life is better. Life is great these days, he thought.

Just at that moment, a car came speeding along the quiet street, not far from Ryan's flat. The black Audi pulled up next to him, and all four doors flew open simultaneously.

'Not so fucking hard now, are you?' shouted John as he and another three men surrounded Ryan.

'All this because I don't want to buy smack? Go fuck yourself.'

'You'll be back on it soon, Ryan; you are weak. You have no willpower.'

Ryan attempted to walk away from John and three others, but they walked in front of him, stopping him in his tracks.

Ryan felt a blow to the back of his head.

'Hello, Mr Walker. Nice to see you are back with us. Don't worry. You'll be just fine.' said the nurse at the side of Ryan's hospital bed.

'What's happened? What's going on? Do my family know I'm here?'

'Your phone was locked, so we haven't contacted any family yet. We don't have contact details for anyone. We only knew your identity from your wallet.'

'How serious are my injuries?'

'You'll be back on your feet in no time. All your vital checks have come back positive, nothing to worry about.'

'Can you call my brother Steven, please? The number is on my phone.'

Chapter 23

'Welcome to London, Luton. Please remain seated until the seatbelt sign goes off and the aircraft has come to a complete halt,' said the air stewardess as they touched down.

Back to the normality of their day-to-day lives. Back to work with no more holidays for some of them until next year, they were suffering from holiday blues as they looked out the aircraft window to see the rain pissing down from a dark grey sky.

'Welcome home indeed. That fucking weather is depressing,' Chelsea moaned.

'Can we not just move to Italy?' Donna joked to the smiles of other passengers, who were now standing in the aisle alongside them.

'What's the plans? It's still early evening. Shall we take the bags home and meet up for a few beers later down The Fox Bar? It's been a while,' said Gary.

'Sound's like a great idea,' replied Donna.

Steven nodded and Chelsea smiled.

As they came out of the airport, the newspaper caught Gary's eye. The front page had photographs of people in red suits in Trafalgar square. They were wearing clown's masks. He didn't say a word but nudged Chelsea, signalling to watch his bag as he dropped it to the floor and walked the few steps to WH Smith's newspaper stand at the entrance.

He picked up the paper and noticed another newspaper had a similar image. This story was everywhere, but what exactly was it? He bought four newspapers and headed back to the others.

'Check this out.' He handed the others a copy of random newspapers. He didn't even know himself.

'Fucking hell!' Donna almost squealed.

'Fucking hell, indeed,' said Chelsea.

Steven and Gary stood against the wall as they read the front-page story. While the group had been drinking strong coffee and as much red wine as they could cope with over the last couple of weeks, the forum had a new organiser but had kept the theme of red coveralls and clown masks going. It had become the recent craze. They had organised protests up and down the UK and as far as France and Holland.

'Look at this!' screamed Chelsea.

She held the newspaper open and showed the rest a collection of photographs from all over the UK. All the people dressed almost the same. Red coveralls and clown masks.

'What the fuck have we missed?' asked Gary.

'Forget The Fox Bar! Let's get some drinks and food as takeaway and come back to my place and get onto this. We can't review this shit sitting in the pub.'

They headed back to Castle Drum. Reading comments to each other from each of the papers, they were in disbelief. They grabbed a few kebabs and pizzas from the local takeaway and twenty-four cans of cider. This was going to be a long night. They had two weeks of media silence to catch up on.

The forum had kept the momentum going, and with millions of the public seeing the original One Show stunt, they had thought it was amazing and decided to join them to carry out peaceful protests. It was reported that close to three hundred thousand people had marched through London the previous Saturday from all parts of the UK. Clown's masks were selling on eBay for anything between one and two hundred pounds. Coveralls were going for around three hundred pounds, and most shops had sold out of both items. It was complete madness, and they had missed it all.

The media had changed their tune towards supporting the people, and most criticised the government, going as far as pointing out historical corruption they knew about, but had sat on for years. Their tactics were straightforward, though. This was to take the heat off themselves. No newspaper wanted their headquarter stormed, so they supported whatever side they thought would win. This was huge, and they felt that the people had a genuine case.

The silence from the government was incredible. They passed a bill that prevented politicians from having a second job, as they knew this would only add fuel to the fire. There was too much scandal developing within the Tory party. It was one disaster after another and a failure in many sectors of society.

Border security was one topic, and the opposition parties had the time of their lives. They pushed for Prime Minister to resign. Although the opposition was just as bad as the Tory party, if not worse, it was a change in government policy that the people demanded, not a change in government. It was a case of better the devil you know.

The group relaxed at Steven's place, stuffed their faces and drank a few Magner's ciders. Each of them were glued to their phones and laptops, discussing what they had found.

'I'm going to log in now,' said Gary.

'There is a post asking where you've been, but just start a new one,' said Steven.

Gary logged in on his laptop and created a post that headlined *I'm back fuckers.'*

After a few minutes, the post had been viewed almost eight thousand times, with countless replies. The majority of the responses took the trend of *You're a fucking hero'.*

'We have done something really amazing,' said Chelsea, as they viewed the same post from different devices.

'I'm going to create a thank you post for everyone. I will need your help with the wording. We did this together, so I think it's only right we all have a say,' said Gary.

After a few minutes, the writing was in full flow; the post was completed, and he hit send on the laptop.

First of all, I want to thank each and every one of you who helped make The One Show a huge success. If it wasn't for the thousands of you who turned up on the night, it would never have been possible. We are deeply grateful for your assistance. You have done this just as much as we did. You all played your part.

The others and I decided it was best to get away for a while and let the dust settle, and we returned to these incredible protests. That was you. Be proud and take it from me that the people's power is working.

Since we started our campaign, we have seen a few politicians forced to resign and good riddance. We have seen changes in the attitude of our media, who are no longer burying stories. In fact, the opposite has happened. They are bringing up historical fraud, and MPs are now shitting themselves in case they are next to be on the front pages. We have done this together.

I'm here tonight, so let everyone know that this is just the beginning. We shall never give up until the government starts listening to the poorer people in society. We will no longer tolerate pensioners deciding if they will heat or eat. We will no longer accept politicians taking cash for questions. We will no longer tolerate expenses fraud. We will no longer accept pay rises for MPs when our public services are stripped. We will no longer take lies from the media. We will no longer tolerate MPs sleeping on the job. We will no longer accept the house of lords, which is a complete waste of money and is undemocratic. We, the people, have spoken. They either listen to or expect us. We will leave no stone unturned to expose corruption.

We have many more stunts to pull off, some dangerous, some criminal and some very funny and embarrassing.

We have so much more work to be done. I ask each of you to tell your friends and family and let this group grow for the better. The media is on our side. We need to grasp this opportunity with both hands and make the most of it. We are coming for you if you are an MP and have skeletons in your closet.

Tonight, I propose another colossal stunt that will make global headlines once more. Details will follow in the coming weeks. We need experts from specific fields, equipment, and more people to be physically involved. Be part of it.

Leave your comments below with any ideas of your own that you can share, and we will get back to you. For now, though, the crew here and I will get drunk and enjoy our evening. You all do the same.

Power to the people!

Midnight Justice.

There were around nine thousand people online at that time; it wasn't possible to read the replies as they came in. Gary closed his laptop and picked up his glass, raised it in the air.

'To the people of the UK and us. To the next successful stunt,' he said as the others clashed their glasses together in a toast to people's power.

Gary and Chelsea headed home and discussed what they would do next. They decided that returning to everyday life for a few weeks was the best thing to do. They planned to forget about things until the planning of the next stunt came up. It was back to the job, cinema, visits to The Fox Bar and to see family. Anything to avoid looking suspicious.

Steven and Donna sat, finishing off the last of their cider. They also gave up looking in the forum. They needed a break. Heading off to bed, Steven picked up the remote control and began watching a movie.

'Is this how it ends now?' Donna asked Steven.

'What do you mean?'

'Well, you have done what you set out to do. You got some kind of justice for old Stanley.'

'We're in the best situation that we've ever been in, so we can't let it slip!'

'Do you have any more stunts in mind? Do you know what Gary is thinking?' Donna cuddled up to Steven?

'Has anyone ever stormed Parliament?'

They had only just slid under the duvet when Steven's phone rang.

Chapter 24

Ryan was whispering.

'They fucked me up, Steven. I'm in the hospital. Not sure what happened, but I'm going to be OK.'

After a brief chat, Steven rang Donna to let her know then headed to the accident and emergency unit.

'Are you OK, bro?'

'Nurse said I will live another day.'

'Who did this, and what's it about?'

Ryan explained that the dealer and his pals now know he has a job and money; they want it and see him as just an ex-junkie who is weak and will eventually be back to what they see as his usual self. After all, Ryan visited them every day of the week for years before his rehabilitation and employment.

'That bastard, John, wait till I get my fucking hands on him.'

'He's not the problem; I can handle him. It's when they are in numbers that's the issue here. They are all nothing when they are alone. John is the leader. The rest are all fucking sheep and terrified of him. He says jump, they ask how high.'

Steven wasn't violent and ensured that extreme violence wasn't involved in their group activities. However, this time, he thought the only way to get the message across was aggression; The problem was that they would always outnumber Steven and Ryan.

'Leave this with me. I think I can get John and his mates to leave you alone.'

This situation was new to Steven. The last time he was involved in any fighting was back at school. He never caused trouble, and luckily trouble seemed to elude him. As Gary was his closest friend these days, he needed to discuss it with him and see if they could develop ideas on the best approach to the situation.

'Take out the ringleader, and the rest will shit themselves. Don't do anything to the others, but let's follow them and wait at their houses. Make our presence felt and then go for John. They will then think that they are next.'

'That sounds like a plan. Put Ryan in the front seat of the car, so they know what it's for.'

'Let's do it tonight, but let Ryan rest. You can sit in the front with me in my car; they know you are his brother. We can call the other lads and have a few cars full. Do you know the others and where they stay?' Gary asked.

'Yes, they all live within a few hundred yards of Ryan. That's why I'm worried about anything happening to him the next time they see him.'

'Give Brad and Andy a call. They'll be up for it. We can easily grab a few other lads for numbers.'

Later that evening, as the sun was going down, they patrolled the streets of Castle Drum, taking guesses where John and his other three associates would gather.

'There's one of them over there,' Steven pointed to the row of shops ahead on the same side as his passenger seat.

'Let the lads know on the WhatsApp group.'

'I've just done that.'

The cars reduced speed to a crawling pace until they eventually levelled with Mick, one of John's so-called henchmen. All four cars had their windows down, and everyone looked directly at Mick. His face went a shade of white. He knew what this was about and looked terrified. He no longer had the luxury of safety in numbers. Steven said nothing but just smiled at him. Gary put his foot hard on the accelerator, and they sped away. The other cars behind followed.

Almost an hour passed. They sat in a car park, close to where they expected another of their targets to appear on his way home.

'Do me a favour, Gary? Don't mention any of this to Donna or Chelsea.'

'Of course, mate. They are on a need-to-know basis, and on this occasion, they don't need to know.'

'It would just make them both worry more, and it's about nothing, really.'

The small talk continued until Andy, two cars behind, sent a message telling them to look behind. Paul, target number two, was almost passing the cars. Just as Paul got near Gary's car, the door swung open. Paul was like a rabbit caught in the headlights. He froze on the spot.

'Not so fucking hard now, are you?'

Gary screwed up his face and grabbed Paul by the shoulder of his jacket. Everyone else got out of the other cars.

'Look, Steven, I never touched Ryan. I was there, but I never got involved. I have no issues with him. It's that psycho John you want and his lapdog Chris. Get them, and you'll be doing the rest of us a favour. He's really fucking lost the plot these days,' explained Paul.

He shook as he looked across the roof of the car.

'Let him go, Gary. I believe him. We just need to go and get the main prize.'

He let go and pushed Paul away aggressively.

'Mick told me that you would be looking for me. He would have told you the same story if you spoke to him. John is picking fights with people daily. It's only a matter of time till he picks the wrong fight.'

'I think that time arrived when he attacked Ryan. Let's go, everyone!'

Gary climbed into the driver's seat.

Time was getting on, and the chances of finding John that night were dwindling. He wouldn't be around late at night without good reason, and the odds that he was home were pretty high, as junkies already had their daily fix.

'Let's knock on his fucking door,' said Brad.

Their cars were parked up side by side, only a few streets away.

'Then there are witnesses. If anything happens, a neighbour could call the police. We are all fucked. I don't want any attention drawn to ourselves.'

'Especially after what we have—' Steven cut his sentence short, as not everyone in the cars knew anything about the group.

'He's there. I'm sure that was him driving past,' shouted Andy.

They proceeded to find the Audi, and sure enough, it was John.

'Brad, you drive ahead and open the gates. If all goes according to plan, we will be there in ten minutes,' announced Gary.

John pulled into the petrol station and began filling his tank.

'We do this right, no fucking about, OK?'

'We got this, Gary,' replied a psyched up Steven.

John paid for his fuel and headed back to his black 4x4 Audi. Two of the lads from Andy's car sneaked into the back of it. As John opened the door, Steven came from behind the fuel pump and punched him on the side of the head. John never saw it coming. He slumped against the driver's door. Gary picked him up and placed him in the back seat with the help of the others. Steven put tie wraps on John's wrists and jumped into the driver's seat, instructing everyone to follow him.

The two lads got back out of the car and proceeded to the petrol station.

'Did you see anything that just happened?' asked one of Gary's associates.

'Never seen a thing; that crackpot deserves all that's coming to him,' replied the cashier with a massive grin across her face.

'So you won't have a problem deleting the CCTV then I suppose?'

'Consider it done.'

The journey was only a few minutes to the planned location. It was a long single-track road with no tarmac or street lighting. Grass grew where the previous tyre tracks lay, as nobody used this road. It was in complete darkness, except for the white dots of moonlight shining through the trees that hung across each side of the path. John was still unconscious when they arrived at the tranquil, dark place on the edge of the forest.

With the metal farm-like gates opened, they entered an abandoned barn. Brad had already made other materials and weapons available, while the others carried John from the car and placed him against an old wooden beam that sat on the floor.

'Pour water on the scumbag.'

As soon as this was suggested, John regained consciousness. It was almost like he was pretending to be asleep.

'Not so fucking hard now, are you?'

Steven grabbed him by the ear and twisted it.

'Is Ryan, OK? I didn't mean for things to go as far as they did.'

John looked up and saw they outnumbered him nine to one.

'Where do we go from here, John? Do you enjoy terrorising people? Do you get some kick from it? Think, you're fucking invincible, do you?' Gary ranted.

'Get his clothes off,' Gary instructed the others.

John lay on the muddy barn floor, naked and shivering. He had no idea what was about to happen or how far these strangers, excluding Steven, would go. Knowing your enemy was one thing, but most of these guys were unfamiliar. Steven whipped a thick rope across John's face, causing his nose to bleed. John let out a massive scream the moment his face began stinging.

'You fucked with the wrong people, John. We will punish you tonight, not just for my brother, but for all the people you have terrorised. It's going to be a long night, John-boy.'

Steven swirled the rope around the air next to John, intensifying his fear.

'Let's waterboard the prick,' suggested Gary.

'No, please! I'm sorry. I'll change. Please let me go. I'll take everything on board and be a better person.'

'I think it's a bit late for that, John. After tonight and we are done, I don't think you will walk again. Or even talk. Let's have a vote, lads. Should he walk or talk tomorrow? Only one of them will happen.'

Gary threw a bag of tools on the floor beside John.

'We could always have fun with that Black and Decker drilling his knees,' suggested Andy

Steven gave him another whip across the naked shoulders, which resulted in more screams. Gary pulled a set of bolt cutters from the bag.

'I'm sorry, I'm sorry. There's no need for this. I will change. I promise.' John began crying.

'Do you lose balance when you lose one toe or all your toes?'

Gary opened and closed the bolt cutters looking directly into John's eyes and eventually smashed it again into the sole of John's right foot. Nobody would ever hear his screams.

'Look, I have learned my lesson. I have a wife and kids at home. I will move away. You tell me what to do, and it's done.'

Tears streamed down his face, dripping off his chin and onto his naked body.

'Here is the deal, John. Do you see my mate over there? He has recorded everything. A scumbag drug dealer, laying naked on a derelict, muddy, abandoned barn floor, pleading for his life. Can you imagine your reputation if this was to go viral?'

'I will do anything. You name it. Do you want money? I can give you money.'

We don't want your drug money, you fucking prick. In fact! I have a great idea. I'm so happy you mentioned that. Do you have twenty thousand pounds handy?'

'No, I have about seven maximum just now.'

'Ok. If we let you go. You will change the bully boy tactics and turn your life around, OK? You will also make an anonymous donation to the local Castle Drum Youth Foundation to help teenagers. Deadline of tomorrow afternoon. Agreed?'

'Yes, yes, anything. Just let me go,' begged John.

'Don't try anything fucking stupid now once we untie you. OK? Remember! Everyone here is just a phone call away, and we can do this all over again if you want. When you next see Ryan, you will apologise, and you will no longer be the bully you have been over the years. Otherwise, I will happily put that drill right through both your fucking knee caps. Do you understand these conditions?'

Steven grabbed him by the chin and looked him dead in the eyes with his rage at maximum levels. This was new to him. He didn't normally get angry.

'Untie him and let's get to fuck out of here!' Gary shouted.

They headed for the cars with John's clothes under Gary's arms.

'Can I have my clothes back?'

'Not a fucking chance. You are lucky we are not torching your fucking Audi. Make sure we get it on video of him going back to his car naked.'

John ran to his Audi and jumped into the driver's seat, shaking.

'Take this warning seriously, you fucking scumbag,' screamed Steven, as he put his head in the driver-side window.

Still shaking and in complete terror, John started his car and reversed out onto the narrow, dark path.

'Thanks a lot, lads. All of you. You don't know how much this means to my brother and me, Gary.'

'It's not a problem, mate. We help each other in times of need. We need these fuckers put in their place. Let me know if he tries anything else and pass on my best wishes to Ryan.'

They walked towards their cars.

Only Steven and Gary went in Gary's car; the rest headed home.

'Remember what I said, Gary. I don't want Donna or Chelsea to know about this.'

'Relax, mate. This will be forgotten about tomorrow.'

'I don't think I have been that angry before. It was something different. I enjoyed it if that makes any sense. It wasn't right, but it's the only way to serve justice to this bastard.'

'Justice was served tonight. Just keep an eye on Ryan and make sure he doesn't go back down the wrong path again.'

Gary dropped Steven off at home. Donna was asleep.

He washed his hands and face and sat on the sofa. He wasn't made for what happened tonight. It was totally out of character. He sat with only a small lamp for light. No TV, no music and thought about the power he had over one of the area's biggest bullies. He liked it and questioned himself if he had done the right thing. Then the overthinking kicked in. What if there was retaliation? What if John didn't take anything on board and just wanted to escape? What if he was ambushed by John when he was with Donna? What if they approached Ryan at the shops? What lengths would he have to reach to make this stop? Would violence become part of him, now that he has experienced it?

Steven switched off the lamp and sat in the dark silence and let his own mind torture him, all from issues that didn't yet exist.

⋯⊷⊷◄❯►⊷⊶⋯